"I'm afraid we're all out of toys,"
she told whoever the newcomer
was, not bothering to look. "And
you probably won't want a
picture."

"On the contrary," replied a deep, masculine and all-too-familiar voice. "I would love a photo. You have got to be the most adorable elf I've ever seen."

Izzy stood frozen in place, at a complete loss for words. She had no question who that voice belonged to. She'd know it anywhere despite all the years that had passed since she'd heard it. Zayn Joffman. As if this day hadn't been bad enough already.

Zayn wanted to swallow back the words the moment they'd left his mouth.

Still, he should have been much more professional. Past history aside, the fact was they were currently business partners, and that precluded flirtatious banter. For better or worse.

Judging by the glaring look of disdain she was currently shooting his way, this particular moment definitely fell in the latter category.

He cleared his throat, aiming for a do-over. "Hey, Izzy."

Dear Reader,

I always wondered what it would be like to work at a winery. I've had the fortune to visit a few recently, and the sights, smells and tastes of those visits still remain with me. Working in such a place as a vintner seems like it would be a dream job. My heroine in this story is not only such a vintner, she finds herself unexpectedly the owner of a successful winery in the heart of wine country, USA. Well, Izzy is only part owner. Turns out she inherited only half her late mentor's winery. The other half belongs to none other than her former love. A man she thought was lost to her forever.

Fate has other plans.

Zayn did the honorable thing years ago when he left his home and everything he knew because it was the best thing he could do for Izzy at that moment. But he's never forgotten her.

Then a shared bequest throws them back together again and Zayn has to wonder if he made the right decision all those years ago.

It was a pleasure to write this story. I hope you enjoy reading it.

Cheers,

Nina

Her Inconvenient Christmas Reunion

Nina Singh

Recycling programs
for this product may
not exist in your area.

ISBN-13: 978-1-335-55651-6

Her Inconvenient Christmas Reunion

For questions and comments about the quality of this book,
please contact us at CustomerService@Harlequin.com.

Harlequin Enterprises ULC
22 Adelaide St. West, 40th Floor
Toronto, Ontario M5H 4E3, Canada
www.Harlequin.com

Printed in U.S.A.

Nina Singh lives just outside Boston, Massachusetts, with her husband, children and a very rambunctious Yorkie. After several years in the corporate world, she finally followed the advice of family and friends to "give the writing a go, already." She's oh-so-happy she did. When not at her keyboard, she likes to spend time on the tennis court or golf course. Or immersed in a good read.

Books by Nina Singh

Harlequin Romance

Destination Brides

Swept Away by the Venetian Millionaire

The Men Who Make Christmas

Snowed in with the Reluctant Tycoon

9 to 5

Miss Prim and the Maverick Millionaire

The Marriage of Inconvenience
Reunited with Her Italian Billionaire
Tempted by Her Island Millionaire
Christmas with Her Secret Prince
Captivated by the Millionaire
Their Festive Island Escape
Her Billionaire Protector
Spanish Tycoon's Convenient Bride

Visit the Author Profile page at Harlequin.com.

To my mom and dad. For all the hard work and sacrifices. And for your continual support.

Praise for
Nina Singh

CHAPTER ONE

You two need each other.

ZAYN JOFFMAN READ the words once more, holding the official document in his hand so tightly, he felt the ache in his knuckles. The solicitor's envelope had contained a personal letter imploring him to understand.

He didn't. Not at all.

Why was he surprised?

He answered his own silent question. Because he was foolish, that was why. Foolish enough to believe that the one member of his family whom he thought to be decent, accepting and kind, was enough of all those things to do right by him in the end. Well, he'd been wrong. And she hadn't done right by him at all. In fact, his late great-aunt had pretty much stabbed him in the back with her last official act as sole owner of Stackhouse Winery in the heart of Napa Valley.

Outside his window, the Manhattan skyline

darkened with threatening storm clouds. The forecasted blizzard couldn't be too far behind. A late-night storm—a harbinger of the mess that was about to come his way.

How very appropriate.

Tossing the letter on the mahogany desk in his study, Zayn rubbed his eyes and tried to take a calming breath. It was bad luck to think ill of the dead, wasn't it? Though, truth be told, he was more disappointed in himself than he was in Great-Aunt Myrna. He should have never for one moment believed that any one of them would deem him worthy enough to be sole heir to any of their holdings. Not even the sole relative who had taken him in. To add insult to injury, he'd have to share his inheritance with someone who wasn't even blood. Of course, Myrna considered the other inheritor family. She always had.

Well, he would figure it out; find a way around this. It would be simple enough to buy the other party out. He certainly had the resources. Despite his family's utter dismissal of him as anyone of any worth, he'd built quite a successful empire all on his own. Nevertheless, people had been underestimating him all his life. If he were honest, he would have to admit he'd given them good reason to do so in his earlier days. Still.

Their total brush-off stung just a bit. Okay. It stung a lot. Surely, they'd all seen how much he'd accomplished over the years, all that he'd achieved for himself. Shouldn't that have been enough to alter their view somewhat?

Turned out the answer was a resounding no—as clearly evidenced by the letter currently lying on his desktop.

Despite his success, his great-aunt's bequest came with a tremendous caveat. He would have to share everything fifty-fifty.

Rubbing his eyes on a weary sigh, Zayn walked around his desk to plop down on the ergonomic leather chair. What's done was done; he would have to move quickly to fix it all. He already had enough on his plate and would have to take care of this matter to move on to more pressing matters.

No, there was no doubt he would have to deal with the current scenario directly and by himself. He had a lot to discuss and negotiate with the other inheritor, and he couldn't trust others to do this for him.

You two need each other.

The written words echoed in his head in Great-Aunt Myrna's voice. He had no idea what she could have meant by that. He certainly didn't need anyone's help to run the place. In fact, he already had a vision for the winery that would be completely at odds with anyone who'd been involved with running it so far.

Stackhouse Winery was too small, too quaint. It didn't even accommodate online orders, for heaven's sake. That meant only mostly locals and a handful of seasonal tourists as customers. Such a setup made no sense at all and was completely unacceptable in today's global economy. The place was way overdue for a massive expansion.

Zayn wouldn't need a business loan to implement his ideas. He had ample resources. Perhaps that was why Myrna had made such an inexplicable decision. She'd probably figured Zayn would be the cash cow that kept the winery running completely as is without tampering with the status quo.

Well, if that was her thinking, she'd been terribly mistaken. And she'd greatly misjudged him.

Pulling over his tablet, he called up his assistant's number in the contact list. She answered before the first ring concluded, despite it being a Saturday morning.

"Clara, I know it's going to be a pain this close to the holidays, but please clear my schedule for the next two weeks. I have to make an unexpected trip to California."

Initially met with a long, silent pause, he realized how totally uncharacteristic his request had sounded.

"Is this regarding the recent passing of your great-aunt?"

Equally uncharacteristic of Clara to ask any kind of personal question.

Zayn supposed it was a rather unconventional time. "In a way," he answered. "The will has finally been revealed."

"I see."

This time Clara's question went unasked, though Zayn could guess what she was wondering. She probably couldn't fathom why he wouldn't just send a corporate representative to deal with the legalities and establishment of his latest acquired asset—or partial asset, as the case may be. He had plenty of qualified MBAs and attorneys on staff who could attend to such matters. And as tempting as it was, Zayn knew sending someone else would simply be the coward's way out. He may have been many things, but he'd never be credibly accused of cowardice.

"We'll be adding another winery to the corporate holdings, it turns out," he told Clara. No need to get into details regarding how he didn't quite own the entire property just yet.

"I see. I'll start the paperwork."

"Thank you. I'm afraid I'll have to personally go see about the acquisition. For various reasons…" He finally answered her unspoken question.

More silence. His assistant would never understand why he had to deal with this himself. How could she? She didn't know the history behind it all. The property wasn't even that large, as she was well aware. Not, at least, when compared to his other holdings.

Clara didn't realize this inheritance was part of his legacy—one final yet slim entry into the world he'd been born to but that had never wanted him.

There was no doubt he would have to deal with the other inheritor directly. The whole situation was one big, sensitive, complicated mess.

Made all the more complicated by the fact that he'd been in love with the other inheritor once long ago.

Santa Claus was most definitely drunk.

Izadora Veracruz had no doubt about it. She just had no idea what she was going to do about it. One thing was certain, she couldn't let Mr. Reyes go through with handing out presents in his current state. Why had he been "in his cups" already? It was barely noon. Though, she knew, day drinking was hardly an unheard-of custom in the heart of Napa Valley.

Still, did he have to be inebriated on this of all days? There was a line of kids in the tasting room at this very moment waiting to sit on Santa's lap for a photo and a small, token gift.

"Why, he's drunker than a rat in a whiskey barrel," Paula said, coming up to stand next to her. They both watched in horror as Mr. Reyes bent to tie his bootlace and nearly toppled over in the process. "He can't go out there, Izzy."

"I know," she responded on a deep sigh. "I can practically smell the fumes on his breath all the way over here."

"You certainly can't let him interact with the children in the state he's in," Paula added, once again telling her what was obviously clear as day.

"I know," Izzy repeated.

"Well, do we have a plan B?" Paula asked.

Not yet. But Izzy would have to come up with one. With Myrna now gone, she was general manager of the winery, and all the responsibility fell squarely on her shoulders.

Correction: she was officially more than general manager now; she was part owner. Not that she expected any kind of help from her "partner." Zayn Joffman couldn't care less about this place. He hadn't been around the winery in years. No doubt he'd assume the role of silent partner and interfere just enough to rub against her nerves.

He'd always been good at doing that.

"I guess I'll have to take care of it myself," she said in answer to Paula's question.

Paula scoffed. "No offense, but you don't exactly fit the description. You'd make a lousy Santa."

She had a point. "Maybe. But I think I can pull off the role of helpful elf." She took her friend/employee by the forearm. "You go tend to Mr. Reyes. Take him to the kitchen and brew some coffee. Strong coffee."

"What are you going to do?"

"I'll go get dressed. I know there's at least one elf costume back there among the plethora of holiday decorations and knickknacks."

Paula gave her a brisk nod and went to do as instructed. Though it didn't appear that a pot of coffee would do much good—Reyes was three sheets to the wind. The man was sure to suffer one monster of a headache in a few hours.

By the time Izzy located and squeezed herself into the elf outfit, she was feeling much less generous toward her irresponsible Santa. For one, the green-felt costume was at least two sizes too small. She'd never been what one would consider petite and her generous curves screamed in protest at the tight confines. Playing Santa's helper had so not been on her agenda for the day.

This event was an annual holiday tradition at Stackhouse Winery. And Reyes had been playing the role of Santa Claus for several years. Why had he picked this day to indulge?

Sighing in frustration—and uttering a silent prayer that the cheap costume material held up for the next couple of hours—Izzy went out to address the children who would almost certainly be disappointed about Santa Claus's absence.

She was right. When she got to the tasting room and greeted the first child, she was met with a resounding frown. No one wanted to have their picture taken with an elf in a too small costume. The token gift would only do so much to tamper the disappointment. More than one parent could be heard grumbling about the waste of time and how they would have to make a trip to the mall.

Izzy could guess what they were all thinking. This was the first event she'd been responsible for since Myrna's passing. And somehow she'd utterly, embarrassingly, failed to pull it off. By the time the last child begrudgingly grabbed his gift and left, it was taking all Izzy had to keep from crying. Not one bottle of wine sold.

She missed her. Myrna had been so much more to Izzy than an employer. She'd been a trusted and solid friend since Izzy was a child, a parental figure who she'd miss forever.

Tearing the elfin cap off her head, she used it as a tissue to wipe her eyes and nose. Damn costume. She could hardly breathe in it. It was going straight into the trash bin as soon as she peeled it off.

The door opened suddenly, letting in a wave of cold air. What now? The tasting room still hadn't been set up, she had to go see about Reyes, and, if she had to spend one more minute in this sausage case of an outfit, she didn't think she could bear it.

"I'm afraid we're all out of toys," she told the newcomer, not bothering to look. "And you probably won't want a picture."

"On the contrary," replied a deep, masculine, and all-too-familiar voice. "I would love a photo. You have got to be the most adorable elf I've ever seen."

Izzy froze in place, at a complete loss for words. She had no question as to who that voice belonged to. She'd know it anywhere despite all the years that had passed since she'd last heard it. Zayn Joffman. As if this day hadn't been bad enough already.

* * *

Why in the world had he said that?

Zayn wanted to swallow back the words the moment they left his mouth. Of course, she looked adorable. She always had. So inappropriate for him to say so, however. There was no excuse for it. He'd just been so thrown off kilter when he'd walked in to find her clad head-to-toe in green felt with pointy-toed slippers. The material hugged her tightly in all the right places. Her dark, wavy hair fell in luxurious waves to frame her heart-shaped face. If anything, she'd grown even more beautiful with time. Though he'd thought he'd been prepared, seeing her again in such an unexpected getup had served to figuratively punch him in the gut. Who knew elves could be so fetchingly sexy?

Still, he should have been much more professional. Past history aside, the fact that they were currently business partners precluded flirtatious banter. For better or worse.

Judging by the glaring look of disdain currently shooting his way, this particular moment definitely fell into the latter category.

He cleared his throat, aiming for a do-over. "Hey, Izzy."

Now that he could clearly see her face, he felt like even more of a heel for the way he'd greeted her. She was clearly upset. Heaven help him, it looked like she'd been crying.

She sniffled. "Zayn."

"Is this a bad time?"

She didn't bother answering but asked a question of her own instead. "What brings you back around these parts?"

He couldn't tell if she was being sarcastic. Surely, she had an idea what had brought him home.

"I'm thinking you can guess the answer to that."

She shook her head. "I don't have a clue."

Still, Zayn couldn't be sure of her angle. She was one of the smartest people he knew. "I'd say we have some business to discuss, wouldn't you? Considering the contents of Myrna's will."

Izzy tapped a finger to her chin, as if contemplating what he'd just said. "Surely the CEO of a multinational corporation doesn't have to fly across the country himself for such a matter. Don't you usually send representatives and proxies to handle your business affairs?"

He shrugged, stepping farther into the room as he removed his gloves and shrugged off his coat. December in Napa was considerably warmer than the Northeast but still held enough of a bite to warrant such winter gear.

"I figured I'd handle this one personally."

Again, she could certainly guess why. "First things first, however. Why are you in that ridiculous getup?"

Izzy made a show of rubbing her hands down her sides and did a little twirl. "Oh, just something I threw on. Besides, I thought you said I looked adorable."

So she wasn't going to let him slide on that. He should have known. "Nevertheless, is there a particular reason one of Santa's elves is playing hooky in Napa during the busy holiday season?"

"There is. It's because Santa himself decided he needed something more festive than java this morning. The same morning he was due to meet and greet kids for our annual Take Your Picture with Santa event."

"So you had to step in as his loyal helper."

She pointed a finger at him. "Bingo."

"Good thing you happened to have a handy elf costume lying around."

She looked down at her midsection. "If only it fit better."

From where he was standing, it looked like it fit just fine.

"Not that it mattered what I looked like," Izzy continued. "The kids were disappointed to get an elf when they were expecting Santa. They didn't seem to think I was all that adorable."

"That bad, huh?"

She nodded, her eyes clouding. "Myrna would have never let this happen. She probably would have called Mr. Reyes last night to make sure he confirmed and that he showed up sober."

"Ah, yes. Myrna Tabor was perfect. I'd forgotten."

Izzy's eyes snapped up to glare at him. "What's that supposed to mean?"

"Nothing. Forget I said it." Izzy had been one of Myrna's biggest fans. And as far as he could recall, the feeling had been mutual.

In many ways, Izzy had been the daughter his childless great-aunt had never had. He, on the other hand, had been the reckless, draining child she hadn't been able to handle.

"Look…" Izzy began, her voice laced with ice. "I know you've had your issues with your family, but Myrna, for one, always tried to do right by you."

That statement was laughable given their current predicament. In all fairness, his great-aunt had indeed done the right thing where he was concerned. Myrna had taken him in and given him a permanent home after years of his being bounced from one to another. But she certainly had *not* done right by him in death. "Let's agree to disagree."

"Fine. I don't have the energy to argue with you anyway. Not after this colossal failure."

Zayn sighed. Such events were exactly the types of things he wanted to eliminate. Myrna and Izzy had thought it important for their role in the community to hold such lighthearted so-called family gatherings.

He couldn't disagree more.

His vision for Stackhouse was much different. He wanted the winery to be a major player in the high-end wine market. His personal brand, known the world over, was exclusive and lux-ury-oriented for the most particular sort of cus-tomer. Frivolous activities meant for kids had no business in a winery that was now part of such a portfolio.

Izzy and his great-aunt had always wanted to run this place like a small mom-and-pop estab-lishment. Cozy and familiar.

He had bigger ideas for it. Ideas his great-aunt had subtly and gently, yet firmly, shot down over the years.

No need to get into all that now.

Izzy reached down to remove the pointy-toed slippers from her feet. Zayn had to force him-self to look away from the shapely, feminine calves. In another lifetime, he'd run his hands down those very same legs. Back when they'd both been barely more than kids. They were very different people now. The whole world was different.

"Where are you staying?" Izzy asked when she straightened.

He gave her a shrug. "I thought I'd stay right here, on the estate."

"That's your right I suppose. Considering it's partly yours." She didn't sound happy about it.

"Don't worry, I don't intend to be in town for long."

She narrowed her eyes on him. "Now, why am I not surprised?"

CHAPTER TWO

WHO KNEW SHE was such a good actress? The very fact that her knees hadn't buckled yet was a true testament to thespian skills she wasn't aware she had.

It hurt to look at him. Zayn was handsome in a way that was striking. Dark hair and piercing black eyes. He wore his hair much shorter now, though he still sported the barest hint of facial hair along his jawline. How often had she teased him all those years ago about his constant and perpetual five-o'clock shadow? The tailored gray suit he wore fit him like a glove, accentuating a toned physique and muscular arms. The overall look was comparable to a model's for an exclusive men's cologne ad. He looked like the international success that he was. Much more polished than the teen she'd fallen in love with, he was the man he had left her to become.

Izzy swallowed the lump of emotion at the base of her throat and willed her pulse under control. She was doing fine on the outside. Calm and collected. All the while inside… Well, her insides were shaking. He was really here, standing before her. Her first love, the one who'd crushed her heart when he'd just up and left town on a sudden whim. She hadn't been enough to keep him nearby.

And despite all of that, every cell in her body wanted to fling herself into his arms, tell him she'd missed him, pretend the last five years had never happened.

How foolish of her. To feel that way when it was clear he was only back because of Myrna's passing. To want his arms around her once more when some of the first words out of his mouth involved leaving yet again…

All this time, she'd thought she'd gotten over him. That he was a large part of her history she'd managed to bury in the past. How very mistaken she'd been. Only fooling herself. It had only taken one look. Just the sight of him brought all those buried feelings of loss and hurt skyrocketing to the surface. But damn if she'd let him know. Especially considering how utterly unaffected he looked himself. While she stood there a roiling ball of emotion.

He was glaring at her after what she'd just said. So she repeated it. "It doesn't surprise me the least bit that you're already talking about leaving when you've only just arrived."

Here it comes, Zayn thought. The recrimination, the accusatory blame.

Izzy squared her shoulders. "I'm not sure exactly why you're here, Zayn. But I'm guessing you don't want to be. You haven't so much as set foot in Stackhouse since you stormed out five years ago."

Zayn hadn't intended their first interaction to be argumentative, but things appeared to be heading in that direction. Par for the course when it came to Izzy Veracruz. Well, if she was looking for a fight, he wasn't about to back down from one.

"I didn't 'storm out,' as you put it. And I hardly had a choice in leaving."

"That's where we disagree."

If she only knew. But this was not the time for enlightenment. Zayn had had his reasons for leaving Napa. And they involved her family just as much as they involved his. Perhaps even more so. It may very well be the one thing they had most in common. A complicated history with their respective families. Only in her case, it had been born of love and concern for her well-being. Whereas his situation had been forged from derision and unacceptance. But he wouldn't be the one to tell her the truth of it all. He'd given his word and he would keep it. As much as it pained him.

He'd have to bear the brunt of Izzy's ire and disappointment to protect the man who'd triggered it five years ago. For the truth of it was, that man had been right to do so.

Izzy gave her head a shake. "Let's not get into all this now. I have to get the tasting room ready for the first visitors scheduled for today. And I can't wait to get out of this confounded costume—which might take a while."

He couldn't even help where his mind went. Zayn had to bite his lip to keep from offering to help her undress. The images traveling through his mind of him doing just that weren't exactly helpful. He had to shift his focus.

"So you're still doing tastings via reservation only, then?" he asked her.

"Yes. That's how we've always done it."

Therein lay the problem. When was the last time this place had any kind of improvement or change? Even the décor was as he remembered it.

A deep, red-hued Oriental carpet lay in the center of the room, the large mahogany table centered atop it. There were still twelve burgundy-velvet chairs placed neatly around the table, though they did appear to have been reupholstered. One wall was lined from floor to ceiling with wine racks, and a black-leather armchair commanded every corner. The various paintings on the walls had changed. But that was to be expected. Myrna had loved to showcase pieces from local artists and to sell their work to interested visitors.

"What of it?" Izzy pressed.

"Let's just say I don't agree with every aspect of how this place is run."

"Is that why you're here? To tell me all the things I'm doing wrong?"

Not so much. He was here to take it off her hands with an offer she couldn't refuse. The idea of the two of them running a winery together was preposterous. He'd tried too hard to forget her. Being her business partner would only pick at the scabs of old wounds. They'd been lovers once. But the past was the past.

Though, she was right about one thing. This wasn't the time or place to discuss all that. He'd just arrived in town, after all.

"Not quite."

Her gaze on him narrowed even further; he felt like a specimen being examined in a science lab. "Then what?"

"Let me buy you lunch when you're done with the tasting. We can discuss some things when we both have time. Does the culinary place still make those rustic sandwiches?"

"As a matter of fact, they do."

"What do you say? Can I buy you a gourmet smoked turkey with soft Brie?"

Her lips tilted to the side. "On a baguette?"

As if he'd forget that's the only kind of sandwich she liked. "Absolutely."

She released a sigh. "All right. Why not?"

"It's a date, then." He flinched as soon as he said the word. It most certainly was not a date. Not like when they were kids and stole every opportunity to sneak off together, either to go to movies, to share a greasy burger from Sal's, or to just lie around the mountainside behind the vines.

She looked down, away from his face. Was she remembering all those times, as well?

"I suppose we do have a lot to go over."

"That, we do," he agreed.

When she looked back up at him, her eyes were sharp and focused. "Why do I get the sense I'm not going to like what you have to say?"

She held a hand up before he could respond, a habit of hers. "Rhetorical question. I'll see you in a couple of hours for lunch." With that, she turned on her heel and walked out, her shapely bottom swaying in the beckon of the tight elf pants. Not that he had any business noticing that kind of thing.

Zayn stood where he was, trying to gather his thoughts. Seeing her again had been as much a punch in the chest as he'd anticipated. Somehow, she'd grown even more beautiful. Or maybe he'd just missed her.

On that disquieting thought, he made his way outside. By the time he grabbed his bags from the rental car and headed for the house, the morning had already grown late.

Going upstairs was like stepping back in time. A large pine loaded with delicate ornaments and tinsel loomed in the foyer by the spiral staircase. Thin garland interwoven with silver tinsel wrapped evenly on the railing and banister. Poinsettias the size of small trees decorated every corner. Just as he remembered from his childhood when his mother had deposited him here with Great-Aunt Myrna before taking off on one of her many holiday excursions.

Her trips abroad grew longer and longer, and consistently became more frequent, until the time she never bothered to show up at all. His father had never been a presence in his life to begin with. Until very recently, Zayn hadn't even heard from the man. The memories resurfaced in his mind like barracuda jumping from choppy waters. His breath caught in his throat and the familiar chill ran up his spine.

Not now. Not here.

Closing his eyes once he got to the top of the stairs, he forced himself to concentrate on the darkness behind his lids and count backward from one hundred. Nausea churned his stomach as his chest pounded. Ninety-eight, ninety-seven...

Blessedly, though it took a while, his breathing resumed to an even, steady pace and his heart rate gradually slowed. The roiling in his gut quieted. That had been close, but luckily short-lived this time. He made himself focus on the afternoon that lay ahead of him. Lunch with Izzy. Their upcoming conversation wasn't going to be the easiest one he'd ever had.

Her parting question echoed in his head. *Why do I get the sense I'm not going to like what you have to say?*

Because she'd always been whip-smart, Zayn answered silently in his head.

And because she knew him all too well.

Get a grip, already.

How many times had she uttered those words to herself since the events of this morning when he'd arrived? Countless. So far, the mantra didn't seem to be working. It had taken everything she'd had to appear calm and unaffected. Cool as a cucumber on the surface.

All the while, inside, she'd been quaking with the shock of seeing him again after all these years.

She'd had no warning. But she had ignored the two emails in her inbox that he'd sent, not ready to deal with the ramifications of Myrna's will. Izzy sighed and smoothed down the skirt of her business suit. The truth was, she hadn't been ready to deal with him. Served her right. She'd have been prepared to face him if she'd known he'd be coming. Bad enough, he'd had to appear during the fiasco with the children and an absent Santa.

Now she had to go out there and commence the wine tasting. But that was good. Her work was like a balm to her soul. Focusing on the wines and presenting them to potential customers would take her mind off her frazzled nerves. She loved introducing Stackhouse wines to visitors. Her job as winery manager was all she could have hoped for.

Heaven knew, she'd given up enough for it. One could effectively argue that she'd given up everything. Her father still wouldn't return her calls. He made himself scarce whenever she visited her parents' home.

Ernesto Veracruz couldn't seem to forgive his

daughter for working at a winery other than the one he'd established.

Now, as she made her way back downstairs and to the tasting room, she felt eternally grateful that she had such a job. And for Myrna for giving her the opportunity. Though she would have never guessed in a million years that, in death, the woman would actually bequeath her half of the winery itself. No, that had definitely come as a surprise. Several days had passed since the estate attorney had announced the news and Izzy still hadn't quite processed the ramifications. Perhaps she never really would.

When she reached the tasting room, Paula was already there setting up. Gone were the scraps of wrapping paper the children had haphazardly thrown around. The Santa chair had been moved back to its spot by the wide stone fireplace. Only a few random bits of glitter remained.

"You're a miracle worker, Paula," Izzy told her, full of yet more gratitude for the woman's sheer competence.

"I'd say you worked quite a miracle yourself earlier," Paula responded. "Averting the crisis that could have been with no Santa to greet the children."

Izzy rolled her eyes. "Hardly—that went about as poorly as it could have."

Her friend gave her a wink and a mischievous smile. "Oh, I'd say it could have gone much worse."

The thought made her shudder. "I suppose."

"And who was that? The tall, dark, handsome looker who showed up? You two seemed very… cordial…"

Paula had no idea about their past history. She'd only been hired a couple of years ago. As far as Izzy knew, the name Zayn Joffman was only one she'd seen on various emails occasionally throughout the years.

Oh, to be so lucky.

"That was Myrna's nephew," Izzy answered.

Paula's jaw dropped. "You mean the one who inherited this place along with you?"

Izzy gave her a nod. "The one and only."

"Huh. I'd seen pictures of him in the past. But, yowzah. That man looks like he could seduce the habit off a nun. No doubt he charms women wherever he goes."

Izzy winced at the description. She knew firsthand just how seductive Zayn could be. And she certainly didn't want to think about just how well he could turn on the charm.

"He grew up in this house, right?" Paula continued. "You must know him well."

Something in her facial expression must have betrayed her emotions judging by Paula's reaction. Her friend clasped her hands in front of her chest with a gasp. "You two were a thing, weren't you? It's written all over your face!"

Izzy did her best to feign an indifference she didn't feel. "Yes, if you must know. Zayn and I were 'a thing.' That was a long time ago, however."

"Well, what happened? Why didn't you two keep in touch all these years?"

"We just didn't."

She knew Paula wasn't going to be satisfied with that kind of an answer.

"Why did you two break up? I mean, you must want to talk about it, seeing as he's back and all."

Did she want to talk about it? Did she want to tell Paula how Zayn had been her first and only love? Or how he'd simply walked away one day never to look back? The way he'd shattered her heart into pieces without so much as an explanation as to why he was leaving?

Zayn had arrived at his great-aunt's house one sunny afternoon when she was twelve and Izzy's life had never been the same. They'd worked the fields together, pelting each other with fat, juicy grapes when the adults weren't looking.

And one day, as she grew older, the playfulness between them had turned into something deeper. It had all come to a head when Izzy had been stood up for her high school prom. Her date had dumped her for the captain of the cheerleading squad after said cheerleader's original date had broken his leg and she'd found herself in need of another one.

So Izzy had turned to her best friend. And Zayn had stepped up to accompany her. Izzy had been the talk of the prom that night, showing up as she had with an older, devastatingly handsome young man.

He'd kissed her for the first time that night and there'd been no going back. Not for her, anyway. Her affection for him had only grown stronger over the years. By the time she was a sophomore in college, she'd been head-over-heels in love.

She'd had her whole future in front of her and was wholly besotted with someone she'd thought had felt the same way about her.

Before it had all come crumbling down around her shoulders.

She shook off the memories to find Paula staring at her, still awaiting an answer. "Zayn decided he wanted something different than what he had living in Napa."

Paula lifted an eyebrow. "Simple as that?"

Izzy nodded. "And then we just sort of lost touch."

In fact, the full truth wasn't simple at all. Not in a way that Izzy had ever understood. For Zayn had left after barely saying goodbye. Totally unexpectedly. He'd given her nothing but a short speech about how he didn't fit in, had never belonged in Napa. How he needed to make his own way far from Stackhouse.

And then he was gone.

A shudder racked through her at the memory of those first few weeks after he'd left. She never wanted to feel such loss again. The loneliness she'd endured without him had nearly broken her.

"Just like that?" Paula asked.

"Just like that."

"Well, it's no wonder you don't date. That man would be a tough act for any man to follow."

Izzy figured Paula might be due for a taste of her own medicine. "And what about you?"

Paula scrunched her eyes. "What about me?"

"I don't exactly see you with a full social calendar. Why aren't you dating anyone?"

"I haven't really thought about it."

Izzy couldn't resist teasing her. "Oh, you haven't? Or is it more because you've been thinking about a certain handsome GP?" Izzy knew for a fact that her friend had a heavy crush on the town's handsome young doctor who'd recently opened his own practice. From what she could tell, the feeling was mutual. Neither one seemed to be doing anything about it, however.

Paula refused take the bait. "We're not talking about me. We are talking about you. Now, I have some more questions about my new boss. Or half boss, as the case may be."

Izzy didn't get a chance to respond as the reserved party of tasters arrived through the front door. She uttered a small prayer of thanks to the timing gods. She didn't really want to answer any more questions about Zayn right now. Not even for Paula, trusted friend and colleague that she was. As it was, she'd had about enough of meandering down memory lane for one morning.

With a wide smile plastered on her face, she greeted her guests and showed them to their seats. The door opened once again, letting in a slight breeze and signaling yet another arrival. That didn't make sense. There were five people reserved for this time slot. And all five were already in place. Two couples and a solitary man who appeared to be in his early thirties.

When Izzy looked up to see who the latest arrival was, she realized she'd thanked the gods much too early. Apparently they weren't quite done playing with her today. Again, she should have known she wouldn't get off that easily.

So much for letting work take her mind off her troubles.

Zayn walked into the room and straight to the tasting table. He'd changed into a black collared shirt and pressed khakis. His dark hair was combed neatly back, though a wayward curl fell lazily over his right eye. Izzy ignored the twitch in her finger signaling a desire to reach for that curl and smooth it back into place.

Pulling out a chair, Zayn nodded to the others in greeting. Then he flashed her a brilliant smile that almost had her knees buckling. "I thought I'd join in. Dying to get a taste of the latest harvest products."

If looks could kill, Zayn figured he'd be good and buried by now. Izzy looked like she was ready to throttle him. In fact, he could have sworn he saw her fingers twitch. Probably itching to wrap around his neck.

"Zayn, what a surprise." Izzy's voice was full of warmth and welcome. If he didn't know her so well, he would have never guessed that she was less than pleased about his presence. He just knew that she was seething under the cool exterior.

"We're only set up for five people," she added.

"Would setting up another spot pose too much trouble?"

The petite blonde next to her with the too tight ponytail seemed to hesitate, her eyes traveling to Izzy's face as if seeking approval.

Izzy responded with a subtle shrug.

"I can set up another spot for him," the blonde said. "It will only take me a sec." She ran to the bar and disappeared behind it. The sound of glasses clinking echoed through the air.

Izzy's eyes flashed with irritation but, to her credit, the smile never wavered.

The blonde returned within moments and efficiently set up a place for Zayn where he sat.

Izzy cleared her throat and began pouring from the first bottle. A deep amber chardonnay fizzed ever so slightly with effervescence as it filled the bottom third of the goblet.

The slender man with the thin wire spectacles was definitely trying to catch Izzy's eye, silently flirting with her. Zayn could hardly blame the poor fool. Izzy was beautiful, graceful and naturally vivacious. And at the moment, she was completely in her element. She was a true professional who knew her craft well. No wonder the guy was looking at her with heart-filled eyes. Even the coupled gentlemen shot her appreciative glances as she spoke. Still, annoyance with the besotted spectacled stranger prickled like thorns under Zayn's skin.

Not that he had any kind of business feeling

what could only be described as jealousy. He'd be a fool to deny that's exactly what the tightening in his chest was about. All these years and his subconscious still figured he had some sort of claim to her. As if he could walk into her life and pick up where he'd left off.

Yeah, right.

One of the women asked Izzy a question. Something about how she'd gotten into this line of work. He hadn't heard the exact words. He'd been too busy focusing on the striking hue of Izzy's eyes that went from dark chocolate to a rich shade of caramel when the sunlight hit her face just so.

Izzy answered right away, almost without thought. As if she was used to receiving the inquiry. She told them her history, of growing up in a family hired to work the vines of a large, established winery, and how she'd fallen in love with every part of the winemaking business. Hardworking and dedicated, she'd gone to school to learn the business end.

She'd been a stellar, accomplished student. Too good for the likes of him. He'd done her a favor all those years ago when he'd left her alone to pursue her dreams. Not that it had been his choice exactly. No. The choice had been her father's.

But the old man had been right when he'd

asked Zayn to leave town and leave Izzy alone. He'd been right that it would be for the best if Zayn stopped seeing his daughter and got far away from her. The old man hadn't been nasty or mean about it. Just straightforward with the clear facts. Izzy was doing great at university; she had a bright future ahead of her. Zayn was spinning his wheels, working odd jobs, and getting arrested for bar fights and other troublesome behavior. He hadn't been in a good place back then. The underlying message hadn't been mean-spirited. But it had been clear. *You're not good enough for her.*

Just like he hadn't been good enough for the parents who'd abandoned him and all the families that had come after. Families ready to get rid of him as soon as they could.

Now, as Izzy reached the part about her college years, she glanced his way ever so swiftly. He caught her eye for the briefest flash. It was enough to send a surge of painful guilt through his core. There was no denying the hurt behind her eyes.

Damn it.

What was the use in feeling guilty? That wouldn't do either of them any good. It was all water under the bridge, anyway. She may not know it but he'd done right by her. The proof was the accomplished, savvy businesswoman standing before him now.

And he'd done right by her old man for keeping that long-ago conversation a secret from Izzy all these years.

She really knew her stuff. And was clearly excited about what she did for a living. All in all, Zayn figured he could have done much worse for a business partner. Too bad the status quo was unsustainable. Never mind the fact that it would drive him insane to try to behave as if they were nothing more than business partners, Izzy would never go along with his vision for the future of this place. And he owed it to himself to pursue that vision. When it came to the one small piece of legacy his family bequeathed him, he wasn't up for negotiating.

One more reason to give Izzy to hate him. As if she didn't have enough already. His hope was that her reaction wouldn't be so bad if he made her a once-in-a-lifetime offer. One she'd be foolish to refuse.

He watched her now as she moved on to the reds. Her hair was done up in a tight chignon, her suit a dark steel-gray—serious, with a sharp collar and high waist, yet somehow feminine at the same time. Still, he had to admit he preferred her in the elf outfit, her hair in disarray under a floppy hat that sported a bell at the pointed tip. Go figure.

"All our wines are aged in red oak barrels," she was saying. "This particular cabernet is especially nuanced by the influence of the oak flavors."

One of the women took a small sip and actually groaned in pleasure as Izzy continued. "Unfortunately, this particular vintage has sold out already. We have a wait list for those who are interested."

"Oh, no!" the groaning woman exclaimed. Other rumblings of disappointment sounded around the table. It all served to prove his point exactly. Exclusivity was one thing. But such a loss of potential sales had to be addressed. As far as he was concerned, there was a failure in the overall process somewhere if a popular wine wasn't available for interested customers. Once he had full control of winery operations, he would definitely address these exact shortcomings.

"We'll make sure to put all your names on the wait list," Izzy assured them, presupposing the future sale. That was something, at least. "In the meantime, please allow me to pour you our pinot noir." She pulled the stopper off another bottle. The reaction to this wine was just as enthusiastic after she poured.

All right. He had to give her that. She had recovered pretty well from what he considered to be a large flaw in their system.

He would be sure to point that out to her right before he told her how he planned to change it all from top to bottom.

CHAPTER THREE

WHY IN THE WORLD had she agreed to this?

Izzy climbed up the makeshift wooden stairs alongside the mountain behind the rows of grapevines. She was still having trouble wrapping her head around the fact that Zayn was actually back in town. She'd fully expected him to dispose of all this with a simple phone call. To tell her what he wanted done now that he was partner, to wish her well and then tell her to send him an occasional email to keep him up-to-date. Then he would leave her alone. Wishful thinking.

He certainly had better things to do, one would think. He'd turned his back on this place years ago, after all.

So her curiosity had gotten the best of her and she'd agreed to this meeting. But why here of all places? If she was smart, she would have insisted on a different location. This spot held too many memories. For her, anyway. Zayn probably couldn't even care to remember the stolen moments they'd spent on this mountainside. Away from the world, away from all those who frowned upon their even being together in the first place. No, he'd probably forgotten all the stolen kisses and gentle touches. That was doubtlessly why he could suggest they have their lunch meeting here of all places, while she was trembling at the thought of being alone with him in this spot.

She found him already setting up at the wooden picnic table when she got there. To anyone observing them, the picture would look like the perfect romantic scene, straight out of some kind of movie about a couple on the verge of falling in love. Zayn had centered a bottle of wine resting in a frosty silver bucket and two goblets at one end of the wooden table. A glass bowl full of some kind of green salad occupied the middle of the table, along with what appeared to be deli-wrapped baguettes. The man sure knew how to treat a woman to a picnic lunch.

Steady, girl. She'd best be sure to remember this was nothing more than a business meeting.

Izzy slowed her gait and forced away the smile that had crept onto her face when she hadn't been paying attention.

"You're here," he announced, flashing her a

grin. He hadn't changed his clothes, unlike her. She'd swapped out the stifling business suit for a comfortable pair of jeans and a thick, velour sweater. But Zayn remained in khakis and the same shirt. Only he'd undone the top two buttons, exposing just enough of the golden skin beneath that she wished she hadn't noticed.

"This looks like quite the spread."

The grin grew wider. "Guess it beats all the wheat toast and soggy hot dogs we used to sneak out here. Back when that was all we could afford."

Did he have to bring up such pleasant memories of their shared past? They surfaced on their own quite well enough without his help. And remembering any of it was the absolute last thing she needed. She'd tried hard all these years to forget.

He'd only been in town a few hours and already her focus was completely shot.

"Yes, well…this definitely beats hot dogs," she said as she sat. "Thanks for running out and getting all this."

"You're welcome. I hope you're hungry."

"Famished," Izzy assured him as she took hold of a napkin and draped it on her lap.

"And thirsty, too, I hope." He grabbed the goblet in front of her and began pouring the wine. A rich, deep sauvignon blanc with a flowery scent she could detect from across the table.

Her stomach rumbled and her mouth watered as she unwrapped the paper from her sandwich.

A girl could get used to this. Delicious food and fresh air in the company of a handsome, attentive man. After the morning she'd had, she deserved to ignore the reality of the situation. Simply enjoying the moment didn't have to mean anything of high consequence. Zayn had gone to a lot of trouble to put all this together, after all. The least she could do was savor the moment.

"Care to sniff the cork?" he asked her before sitting on the bench across the table from her.

"That won't be necessary." She took a bite of the baguette and nearly moaned out loud at the burst of flavor along her tongue. Homemade French bread would always be her great weakness. These days, lunch usually consisted of a granola bar eaten hurriedly at her desk as she ran over numbers or processed orders. This was definitely a treat by comparison.

He really did appear to be trying here.

Whatever was to happen with their partnership, she had to give Zayn the benefit of the doubt. They'd been barely more than kids when he'd left; they were both older and wiser now. And what he'd done by bringing her this meal was clearly an olive branch of sorts. They could approach the upcoming days as two mature and reasonable professionals who only wanted what was best for Stackhouse.

"Thanks again, Zayn. This sandwich is to die for. It almost makes up for the morning I had."

He took a small sip of wine. "You're welcome."

"Mr. Reyes was deeply apologetic, by the way," she began by way of conversation. "Swore it wouldn't happen again. Next year, he'll be completely dry and properly sober. Downright Santa-like."

Something shifted in his eyes right before he cleared his throat. "Next year, huh?"

She nodded, took another bite, this time making sure to get a good chunk of avocado along with the bread. "Yes. There's always a Santa visit just as there's always the annual light show through the vines."

"That's part of the reason I wanted to have this discussion," Zayn said, putting his sandwich down to methodically run his fingers along the stem of his wine goblet.

Something stirred in the lower pit of Izzy's stomach. Her libido resurfacing after many dormant years. So very inconvenient. She forced herself to focus on the conversation.

"What? About Mr. Reyes not getting drunk

next year? He assured me he won't." She braced herself, ready to go to the mat to fight for the older man if need be.

"About all of it, Izzy."

Izzy swallowed the morsel in her mouth. The tone of Zayn's voice and his granite expression suddenly had apprehension fluttering in the center of her chest.

"All of what?" She put her food down and wiped the corners of her mouth with the paper napkin. "Maybe you should just come right out and tell me, Zayn. Why are you really here? Why have you come all this way?"

He tilted his head. "All right. I came to make you an offer."

"What kind of offer?"

Before she could process what he was doing, he slid his smartphone across the table toward her. The screen showed a series of numbers with a dollar sign.

"That's a lot of zeros. What do they mean?"

"It's my starting point. We can negotiate, but I think it's more than fair."

"Fair?" Her mind had somehow gone numb. Was she really hearing and understanding him right? His next words confirmed that she was.

"I'd be willing to write you a check right now with that amount on it. For your half of Stackhouse."

All thoughts of civility and mature discourse fled her mind and the blood chilled in her veins. What a fool she was. This lunch, the picnic table, the wine. She thought he'd gone out of his way to do something nice for her. Ha! What a joke. It was all just a way to butter her up before he dropped the bomb.

She should have known better.

He would never understand her. Not in a million years. Her whole expression went from calmly serene to hardened and angry. She looked ready to fling the wine in his face. Or to throw her sandwich at him. Probably both.

He'd known she wasn't going to be thrilled with the idea. But she could have bothered to at least listen to him for a minute or so.

"You have got to be kidding me." Her tone held a glacier's worth of ice.

He held a hand up. "Iz, just hear me out."

"Don't call me that!"

He hadn't even consciously thought to revert to his pet nickname for her. He took a deep breath. "Fine. I won't. But can you just take a minute and listen to reason?"

"Reason? Is that what you call it?" She threw her arms wide and gestured around. "Is that why you went to the trouble of doing all this?

The expensive wine, picking up a gourmet lunch the exact way I like, setting up a picnic."

Heaven help him. Were her eyes growing shiny? She was so mad at him, she was tearing up.

"Is that why you did all this?" she demanded to know. "So you could set up the scene to try to sweet-talk me out of my job?"

Out of her job? He had no intention of asking her to leave. The place would be lost without her. She was jumping to all sorts of conclusions. In all fairness, he probably could have handled the delivery of the message a bit better. Usually, he prided himself on being a master communicator, one who could negotiate and barter with outstanding results. But he was totally off his game here. Between seeing Izzy again and being thrust back into the memory trap that was his childhood home, he was completely off balance.

"Look, no one said anything about your job being in question. No matter what happens, you know you have a spot here. In fact, I'd love for you to continue on in your role."

Her lips thinned into a slim line before she spoke.

"Oh, you would, huh? Last I checked, you weren't the sole decision maker."

"That's the problem, Iz—" he caught himself

"—*zy.*" The elongation only served to make her name sound even more endearing.

She bristled some more. "What's that supposed to mean?"

"You and I both know we have very different ideas about how this place should be run. You and Myrna ran it like a community social center that happened to sell some wine through some very narrow channels. That's no way to run a winery. Or any business, for that matter."

"I find that highly offensive. That way happens to work for us. It has been working for us."

He shrugged. "It isn't meant to be. I'm simply stating the facts. We are going to keep butting heads if we remain co-owners."

"What if I was the one who said I wanted to buy you out?"

He tried not to give anything away of his reaction to that so-called threat. They both knew Izzy didn't have those kinds of resources. He remained silent, figuring that was answer enough.

She waited several beats before continuing. "So, your brilliant scheme to address our differences is to buy me out. Is that it?"

"I think it's a very sound, reasonable plan."

"But you'd have me remain on board as a voiceless employee who has no say in operations and is there simply to follow your directives? Do I have all that straight?"

When she put it that way… "Izzy, of course you'd have a say. You'd still be vineyard manager."

"Only by your good graces. And I can just guess how much weight my actual opinions would hold." She shook her head. "Why?"

He thought he'd explained his reasoning pretty well. Though clearly she didn't agree with it. "Why what?"

"Why did I think you might have changed?"

So now she was going to bring up past history? He didn't have to defend himself to her or to anyone else. The truth was, he had indeed changed. But no one back here would ever see that. Not Izzy. And most certainly not her father.

Well, he was done explaining himself to anyone. He'd made that decision years ago. Fighting to redeem himself in others' eyes had led to nothing but frustration and futility. Despite all his professional success, everyone in his past refused to see him as anything more than the angry, punk teen who constantly found himself in trouble. Such an embarrassment. Why would he think Izzy would be any different?

Her next words confirmed all the thoughts running through his head.

"You're still the same selfish man who thinks of no one but himself."

* * *

Stupid. Stupid. Stupid.

To think, she'd felt touched that Zayn had gone out of his way to treat her to a pleasant lunch. For a second there, she'd thought he might have actually been interested in catching up. That he might have been curious about how she'd fared since he'd left. All the while, he'd had the most crushing of ulterior motives. Well, it was her fault for feeling even one iota of hurt. How often could she be so foolish and deluded when it came to one man?

Five years ago, he couldn't wait to get away from her. Now he couldn't wait to get rid of her. This winery and the estate it sat on was her home, her refuge. What did he think she was going to do with her life if she walked away from it? And he had to know she would have no choice but to walk away if she took any of his money for her half of it.

Now, as she made her way to the cellars, she had to consider the possibility that his intention all along was to get her to leave and pretend he'd given her any kind of option.

She wasn't surprised when she heard footsteps behind her as she inserted the glass testing tube into one of the barrels.

"Look, I didn't mean to blurt my intentions out so bluntly that way. It was wrong of me to just throw it at you. I apologize." A bag of lavender candy materialized in her line of vision. "A peace offering. I picked it up for dessert from the culinary school shop. I hope you still like these things?"

Oh, no. She wasn't falling for that again. Tokens from the past were not going to work anymore. Fool her once and all that.

"I have a lot of work to do, Zayn."

She ignored the candy and heard his deep sigh behind her. He pulled his arm back when she didn't take the peace offering. "We have to address all this, Izzy."

Izzy gripped the tube so tight her fingers ached. He was right. As much as she wanted to slam the proverbial door in his face and walk away, logic dictated that she couldn't ignore him. Myrna had really put her in such a hard predicament. She'd known the woman her whole life. Myrna had never made any kind of decision without thinking it through completely. She must have had her reasons for setting up her will the way she had.

You two need each other.

Those words had been the end note of the letter she'd included for Izzy in her will. Izzy had no idea what she might have meant by them.

Why would she need the man who'd left her high and dry with a broken heart? It had to be a reference to Zayn's business acumen combined with her own intimate knowledge of Stackhouse. Myrna must have thought the two of them could work together in her absence. Or maybe Izzy was just grasping at straws. One thing was for certain—she had to deal with Zayn until they settled all this. One way or another.

Sighing, she turned to face him.

"I'm really sorry, Izzy. I didn't mean to upset you." He sounded sincere enough. He held out the bag of candy once more. This time, she reluctantly took it. But she refused to thank him. "I'm usually better at bringing up negotiations. It's just, you started talking about the Santa Claus winery visit and then the light show, and I figured it was a good segue."

"And you have an issue with such events?" she asked rhetorically.

He shrugged. "I don't see how they would work as any kind of marketing strategy to drive up sales. But I should have stated my point better. I know Myrna enjoyed such get-togethers."

"Look, this isn't exactly easy on me, either," she began, trying to keep her voice steady yet firm. "But Myrna wanted me to have half this place. She must have had her reasons." Probably because the older woman had guessed that her great-nephew would swoop in and lay rough-shod waste to all that Stackhouse represented and stood for in Napa Valley. It was so much more than just a winery, but Zayn would never see it that way. All he saw were dollar signs.

"You are so focused on the numbers," she added.

"We can talk about the amount I'm offering you."

He'd misunderstood her. She resisted the urge to fling the candy bag in his direction. "This has nothing to do with your offer!" How could he possibly be so obtuse?

Zayn gave a slight shake of his head. Heaven help them both, he really didn't see it. "Then what?"

"Think about it. Myrna could have just given me a monetary amount as her operations manager. And stipulated as part of your inheritance that you keep me on board. But she didn't do that."

He lifted a shoulder. "And? What's your point?"

"Her decision to do things this way was about more than just making sure I'm taken care of." Izzy felt a tightness in her throat as she said the words. For there was no doubt Myrna would have done just that: made sure Izzy was well taken care of after she was gone. But the way the older woman had drawn up her will, Izzy knew she was asking for something from her, as well. To make sure the winery stayed the way it was, numbers be damned.

"She'd had a vision for this place since the moment she'd taken it over once your uncle passed."

He crossed his arms in front of his chest, studied her. "And she knew you would guard that vision."

Izzy nodded. Maybe there was some hope that he could understand.

"Then why did she even bother leaving part of Stackhouse to me?"

Wow. Izzy felt torn between shaking him and the sudden unexpected urge to hug him. For Zayn to even ask that question was downright heartbreaking. Just went to show that he really hadn't come to grips with his past despite all the years that had gone by.

"Because you were her great-nephew, Zayn. And because she loved you."

His only answer was to scoff at her words before silently turning around and walking away. She knew better than to try to go after him.

CHAPTER FOUR

WELL, THAT HAD gone about as poorly as it could have.

Zayn made his way back to his suite completely unaware of his surroundings. Somehow it was afternoon already, but it felt like weeks since he'd arrived. The familiar pounding in his chest taunted him, but he figured if he got back to his room in time and shut the door behind him, he'd be able to keep it at bay.

Izzy had no idea what she was talking about. Aunt Myrna may have given him a home, but any notion of love or affection was definitely a stretch of the imagination.

Izzy had always seen the best in his great-aunt. The admiration had been mutual. Myrna'd had a soft spot for Izzy since the day her family had started working this vineyard. The little girl had skipped right into his aunt's heart upon arrival. Eventually, Myrna had become Izzy's mentor. And Izzy had been an eager protégé.

Izzy was the bright spot in their lives back then. Whereas he'd been nothing but a dark cloud looming overhead.

Ninety-six...ninety-five...

By the time he reached fifty, to his relief, his breathing started to steady and his heart rate gradually slowed as he finally reached his room. Within moments, his cell phone alerted him to an incoming call. The screen told him it was Clara, his assistant in New York. She'd left several messages. He hadn't had a chance to call her back.

Begrudgingly, he answered the call, though more talking was the last thing he wanted to do at the moment.

"Hey, Clara."

"Hello," came her crisp, efficient voice from the other side of the country.

"Sorry I haven't been able to call back. Things haven't gone quite the way I'd planned."

"Oh? In what way?"

He could just picture her eyebrows raised clear to her hairline. "The negotiation isn't going well."

"I see. The other party is driving a hard bargain, then?"

"Yes." *And no*, he added silently. Izzy wasn't interested in any kind of bargain whatsoever.

"At the risk of sounding indelicate," Clara began, "she isn't family, is that correct?"

The question threw him off. Izzy wasn't family by blood. But in every other sense she was. "Not technically. Why do you ask?"

"Well, there may be other avenues we can pursue to acquire the entire property."

He had a feeling where she might be going with this. Clara could be like a pit bull with a bone when it came to business. Such a trait was one of the reasons he'd hired her three years ago. But her instincts were highly misplaced in this case.

"I don't think we need to go there, Clara."

Still, she pled her case. "Your great-aunt was old and frail. Perhaps not in her right mind. Someone close to her could have easily taken advantage of her frailty and old age."

Zayn had to bite his tongue to keep from laughing out loud at the suggestion. As if anyone could have taken advantage of his great-aunt. As for Clara, she was simply doing what she was paid to do: figure out what was best for the company and determine how best to achieve it.

"Not an avenue I'm willing to pursue."

"Are you certain, Mr. Joffman? It probably wouldn't even have to go to court. Usually such matters are settled outside of a courtroom."

"Not an option, Clara," he said with more steel in his voice than he'd meant to. Such an idea was out of the question. He wouldn't even entertain it for a moment. Izzy was the last person in the world who would have taken advantage of anyone, let alone his aunt. She'd worked hard at Stackhouse over the years and deserved what Myrna had bequeathed her. It was simply pure, rotten luck that they had such different ideas about how the winery should be run.

He began to explain. "It just so happens that the other inheritor happens to be an honest and valued member of the community. She doesn't have a manipulative bone in her body. I've never seen her so much as tell a fib. And I've known her a long time."

Clara didn't speak for several beats. When she did, she sounded surprised. "I apologize. I didn't realize you knew the other person so well."

Zayn couldn't help but wince at the last word. If Clara only knew how accurate a statement she'd just made. He and Izzy had known each other intimately, all right. Though that seemed like another lifetime ago. Especially now.

"No need for apologies," he assured his assistant. "Trust me when I say a resolution is forthcoming. We just happen to be in a holding pattern at the moment."

Luckily, she didn't press further or ask for any more information. "Then I will await further instruction and file the matter away for now."

He thanked her then powered off the phone. He needed some quiet time to think things through. What he'd said to Clara just now was the absolute truth. Izzy didn't have a manipulative bone in her body. In fact, the only character flaw of Izzy's he could even think of was that she could run a little hot-headed. Other than that, she was near perfect.

Izzy was the full package. Smart, hardworking, attractive as a siren. An image of her wearing the sexy elf costume flashed in his mind and he had to mentally swat it away. When she smiled, it was like a mini sun rising to brighten any place she happened to be. Was she seeing anyone? he had to wonder. Not the first time he'd pondered that particular question. She had to be. She was too good a catch. Any man on earth would be lucky to have her.

Damn. He didn't need to pursue that train of thought. Zayn rubbed his forehead and plopped down on the bed behind him. He had it bad still, didn't he? He'd managed to avoid facing it all this time, thanks to the physical distance between them. But his feelings for Izzy had never diminished. All it took was setting eyes on her again to bring them all to the surface.

He hadn't the slightest idea what to do about it.

"I don't see why these aren't lighting up."

Izzy stared up at Ethan Greaves, MD, as he stood on the stepladder in front of an animated Frosty the Snowman. The winery light display was almost complete. But there appeared to be a glitch in this particular section. Frosty was completely dark.

"Well, what's your professional diagnosis, Doc?" she asked him. Ethan was a true and loyal friend who took a day off every year from his busy practice to help Izzy and Myrna set up the mile-long display through the main part of the winery past the estate and down to the vines. All he accepted in payment was a case of cabernet and a homemade lunch. Izzy was grateful for his Christmas spirit. Particularly this year with Myrna gone and the return of the prodigal son.

Ethan draped the wires he was holding over the top of the ladder and stepped down. He answered her question with mock seriousness. "I'm afraid it's not looking good."

"Just give it to me straight. I can take it." Her reply was delivered in an equally solemn voice.

Ethan shook his head, his features cut in stone. "All right. But brace yourself."

She nodded fervently. "I'm ready."

He took a deep breath. "We're going to have to replace all the bulbs and restring the snowman."

Izzy gasped with exaggerated flourish and clasped a hand to her chest. "Is there really no other way?"

Ethan took her by the shoulders, continuing the playful charade. "I'm afraid not."

"Oh, no!"

His grip on her shoulders tightened ever so slightly. "I know this is hard. But you have to be strong, Izzy. For him. For Frosty."

That did it, the sheer gravity in his voice served to undo her playacting. She burst out in laughter, unable to hold it in any longer. Ethan chuckled along with her.

She felt Zayn behind them before she saw or heard him. A sensation of awareness had shivered along her skin, alerting her to his presence.

"Am I interrupting?" Zayn wanted to know.

Ethan turned to him, his hand extended. "Z-man! I'd heard rumors you were back in the valley."

Izzy watched as the two men shook hands. Zayn appeared cordial enough, said all the right words to the town doctor he'd been casually acquainted with before leaving Napa. But she could sense an undercurrent within him. He was displeased. She could just guess why.

He was unhappy about the light display. No doubt, he saw it as yet another unnecessary holiday feature the winery put forth every year at this time.

Had the man always been such an insufferable Grinch?

"No, you're not interrupting." She answered his earlier question, adding, "We were just working on reviving good old Frosty here. It appears he needs some new equipment."

Zayn quirked an eyebrow at her. "Maybe that's a sign?"

She decided to play devil's advocate. "What kind of sign do you think it might be?"

Zayn released a weary sigh and plunged his hands into his pants' pockets. "Is all this really necessary, Izzy? What does a winery in California need with a holiday light show? It has nothing to do with selling wine."

She knew it! "You can't be sure of that. At the least, it drives more traffic to the winery. This time of year isn't exactly hopping with tourists." She glanced at Ethan for some backup. But he simply stood there, glancing from her to Zayn, as if watching an entertaining tennis match. A small, amused smile hovered along his lips.

Clearly, there would no assistance forthcoming from that corner.

"You may have a point. But it's not the kind of traffic we need, I would gather. Families with small children are typically not big buyers. A bottle here and there."

She crossed her arms in front of her chest. He really wanted to argue this here and now. "It's better than nothing," she countered.

"Is it? Compared to the cost, I'd say it's not much better at all. The electricity bill alone is probably a nonstarter."

Izzy gritted her teeth. "The entire community loves that we do this. It's the only light display of its kind within miles. There's no way we're canceling it." Not as far as she had a say.

Ethan cleared his throat. "I guess I should head out, then."

So now he was abandoning her altogether? Izzy thought. Men! They were all frustrating, undependable creatures. "Where are you going?" she demanded, her tone unintentionally vehement.

Ethan raised his hands. "I was going to try to locate some replacement bulbs. To see if we can find the dead spot in these lights."

Zayn tilted his head, stared up at the sky. He appeared every bit the part of a man trying to wrangle the last of his patience. "Fine. If you insist on doing this, let me have a look. I took a couple of electrical engineering classes in college."

She hadn't known that about him. Why would a businessman have taken engineering classes? "You did?" she asked, unable to mask the curiosity.

Zayn shrugged. "Elective. I've always been interested." He stepped over to Frosty to study the frame. "I'll just take a look."

Ethan stepped aside. "Go ahead, if you wish, but I've been trying for the better part of half an hour. It's not lighting up."

Zayn climbed a couple of steps and grasped the wires, examining them. He unscrewed one of the bulbs and examined it, as well. "Nothing appears to be broken."

He climbed all the way to the top of the ladder, still holding the wires. "I think I see the problem. It might be—"

Nothing could have prepared her for what happened next. Zayn suddenly went still, as if frozen in time. She could only watch in horror as his body rocked head to toe with a sudden shudder. In the next instant, he toppled off the ladder and landed with a thud on the dirt.

CHAPTER FIVE

BAH, HUMBUG.

Zayn awakened to a beam of light flashing in his eyes. First the right, then the left. When the light lowered, he saw Ethan Greaves's face hovering near his. And he could detect the scent of lavender. That must mean Izzy was nearby. She always smelled of lavender. Or was it vinegar? No, that didn't sound right. It must have been *lavender*; that had to be the correct word. It seemed to sound better.

Clearly, he'd hit his head.

"What happened?"

"Must have been a faulty wire," Ethan answered. "You took some current through your body."

"Huh."

"The electric shock had to have been minor," the other man added, "but you hit your head in the fall."

Bingo. He'd been right. As if to confirm, the

pounding behind his forehead chose that moment to register. A small groan of agony escaped his lips.

"Oh my God, Zayn! Are you all right?" He fought past the pain to turn and focus on Izzy's concerned, worried face. She sat next to him on her haunches, her arm around his shoulders.

"Sure, I am." He sniffed the area at her neck. "You smell like vinegar."

Her eyebrows scrunched together. "Huh?"

He must have said the wrong word. "Never mind."

"At least you had the presence of mind to fall where there was a doctor standing near you," Ethan told him.

"Lucky for me." It seemed Zayn's talent for sarcasm superseded head trauma.

"I think you'll be okay. Can you stand? Nice and easy."

With help from both of them, Zayn managed to get to his feet. Aside from a seesaw effect where the scenery in front of him tilted first one way then the other, he didn't feel too off balance. The pounding remained, however, and Zayn's vision was slightly out of focus.

"How're your eyes?" Ethan asked.

"Fine," he lied.

"Let's get you inside the house."

"Zayn, I'm so sorry," Izzy was saying under his left ear. "I will never forgive myself for this."

It wasn't her fault Frosty had taken offense to the way Zayn had manhandled him. He heard Ethan chuckle next to him and realized he'd said the words out loud.

"So glad your sense of humor wasn't damaged in your fall."

Several moments later, Zayn found himself semicarried into the front foyer of the house and settled on the large circular sofa.

Ethan stood with his hands on his hips as Izzy hovered over Zayn, adjusting the pillow behind his head. "Does it hurt very badly?" she asked.

"Don't worry, Izzy. It's fine." Another lie. The pounding was wreaking havoc behind his skull. He wasn't about to tell her the truth, however. His masculine pride had taken enough of a hit for one day.

The concern in her eyes didn't fade. She realized he was being dishonest; she knew him too well.

"Take something over-the-counter for the pain," Ethan instructed him. "I don't think you have a concussion, just a little jostled. Still, I'd like you to follow concussion protocol for the next forty-eight hours."

"What's that mean, exactly?" Izzy asked.

"No screens whatsoever. No reading. A dark room if you can."

Great. There went any hope of getting any work done while he was here in Napa. He was already behind on more than one major project. Maybe he should have never come. His Manhattan penthouse suited him much better than a sprawling estate mansion on any given day. He should have known nothing good would ever come from his coming back home. Now he was laid up with a huge goose egg on his head. Things couldn't possibly get any worse.

"You have to keep an eye on him, Izzy."

"I do?" she asked the exact moment Zayn asked, "She does?"

Correction: things had definitely just gotten worse. As if toppling off a ladder in front of her hadn't been bad enough, now he'd be beholden to Izzy.

Ethan shrugged. "Someone does. To monitor his pain and note if it gets any worse. And to make sure he doesn't have any balance issues when he does need to get up. The last thing he needs is another tumble."

Izzy nodded. "Of course." She'd said it without hesitation but Zayn had noticed the apprehensive swallow before she'd answered.

This all served him right. The only reason he was here laid up on this couch was that he'd behaved like a heartsick teenager filled with envy. He'd been in the middle of attending to some urgent emails when he'd foolishly looked out his window and seen her and Ethan working on that blasted display. He'd tried to ignore them, but it had proved futile. He'd finally given in to the urge and opened the window to hear snippets of their conversation. Lots of banter, plenty of laughing. Clearly, she enjoyed Ethan's company, unlike his own. Like a fool, he'd made his way downstairs and outside before he'd had a chance to think about why exactly he was doing so.

Then, to top it off, he'd tried to play the hero who could fix the electrical issue. Only to land on his back on the hard, stony ground. Not his finest moment. And Izzy had been witness to it all.

"I don't need a babysitter," he argued now. "I know how busy Izzy is. The last thing she needs is to hang around here and nurse after me like I'm some kind of invalid."

Ethan shook his head. "That's not how this works, buddy. I remember you being hard-headed, but not quite that hard. Someone needs to be by your side at all times for the next two days. Doctor's orders." His voice was firm.

Zayn opened his mouth to try to argue some more but Izzy held a hand up to stop him in that signature way of hers that he found both endearing and maddening at the same time. "I'll do it. It won't be a problem. I can take a day off of barreling. I'll just have Hector come by and help tomorrow when he's back in town. He's been away on business."

Hector was her brother. The same brother who had good-naturedly but relentlessly teased him when they were all youths. Zayn had given back in equal measure, but Hector was truly talented at leveling bona fide A-plus insults. He'd have a field day once he got a load of how Zayn had ended up in his current predicament.

Yep, things were just getting better and better by the minute.

Zayn could hear their muted conversation when Izzy walked Ethan out several moments later. The other man seemed to reassure her, his voice low and calming. His bedside manner was certainly not lacking.

She returned with a couple of painkillers for Zayn. "He's going to call one of his patients who happens to be an electrician to come fix whatever's wrong. A real electrician," she added after a beat and then handed him the pills.

Good ol' Ethan to the rescue. Again. "Ouch."

She startled. "What? Is it the pain?"

"No. Just another blow to my pride."

A smile appeared to tickle her lips. "Sorry.

Couldn't resist. What were you thinking, anyway? Handling a live wire."

I was thinking how much I hated seeing you enjoying yourself basking in another man's charm and had to make a fool of myself as a result.

"Thought I could help," he said instead. "Not like I knew it was live."

"Hmm. Despite all those electrical engineering classes."

Harsh teasing apparently ran in the Veracruz family. "You know this is hardly necessary," he told her now that the doctor had left and the two of them were alone. "You certainly don't have to stick around and play nursemaid. I'm feeling better already."

To prove it to her, he lifted the quilted cover she'd thrown over him and made a move to stand. Only to discover he wasn't as steady on his feet as he'd hoped. The floor seemed to give out from underneath him and he stumbled backward.

Izzy rushed to his side and threw her arms around him in some kind of effort to stop the mishap. The end result was that both of them ending up haphazardly on the couch, Izzy sprawled on top of him. It took all his will not to reach his arms around her and pull her tight up against him. She felt so right where she was, like she belonged right there on his lap. Her soft skin radiated warmth in every spot their bodies were in contact. The smell of her shampoo, a light delicate scent of vanilla, tickled his nose and made him want to nuzzle his face into her thick, luscious hair.

Lavender and vanilla, the combination was delectable and oh so familiar.

All too soon, she scrambled off him and stood, before backing away several steps. "Would you stop being so stubborn?" she demanded. "You could have hit your head again on the back of the sofa."

"Aw, you sound like you might care what happens to me." He couldn't resist the taunt.

She gave a small shrug of her shoulders. "I would hate to have to explain it if my newly minted business partner up and died on my watch. Too many questions."

"Right. That would indeed look suspicious, especially given the topic of our last business discussion." Hard to believe they were joking about the very thing that threatened to further strain their already complicated relationship. But there it was.

"My point exactly. Now, would you please try to get some rest?"

"I can't. Too fidgety. I'm not used to sitting around."

"You can watch me bake cookies, I suppose. Though I guess I'll have to do it in the dark, given how you're concussed."

"You're baking cookies?" It occurred to him that he didn't normally date the type of women who baked cookies. Not that he particularly cared about that sort of thing.

"Dozens and dozens. I was going to stay up all night to do it, but looks like I don't have to now."

"Why so many?"

"The light display goes live tomorrow. We always have fresh-baked sugar cookies to accompany the hot cocoa the first night."

Zayn couldn't help his snort. "Still insist on going through with that, do you? Despite…you know, this." He gestured to himself and then pointed to the goose egg on his head.

"If the electrician gives us the okay. Why not?"

"I could give you several reasons why not."

"You can sit out there and greet everyone with me. The main tent is heated. Who knows? You might even enjoy some yuletide cheer."

He laughed at that. "Highly unlikely."

She slammed her hands on her hips. "What exactly do you have against the holidays, anyway? I know you were never particularly excited about Christmas, but now you seem to have reached a Grinch-like level of disdain for all of it."

"Come on, Izzy. You know we never really celebrated the way you did with your family."

Something flashed behind her eyes that he couldn't quite place. But it was gone in an instant. Perhaps he had imagined it.

He continued. "First of all, it was usually only me and Myrna. And she was always much too tired this time of year to do anything more than hand me the present she'd picked out for me. Then she went off to rest and I watched cheesy Christmas movies for about twelve hours straight." To Aunt Myrna's credit though, she'd been the only one who'd even tried to celebrate any kind of holiday with him.

Izzy knew all this—why had she insisted on bringing it up?

"You know you were always welcome to spend the holidays with us."

"I know. Believe me, the times I did that were the only pleasant memories of Christmas I can recall whatsoever. So, thanks for that. And thanks to your mama and papa, too. How are they, by the way? I've been meaning to ask."

The same dark shadow crossed her eyes before she looked away again. "Fine. They're both fine."

The hint of a waver in her voice kept him

from asking anything more. Something was off about the way the conversation had turned and he didn't have it in him to try to speculate, the pounding in his head having not quite subsided enough.

In any case, it appeared the conversation was over, anyway. She suddenly reached her arm out and waited for him to take it. Then she helped him stand. For one insane moment, he wanted to pull her down onto the sofa with him instead.

"Well, if you're not going to try to get any rest, you may as well come with me to the kitchen. I have some baking to do."

CHAPTER SIX

IF SOMEONE HAD told her a week ago that Zayn Joffman would be sitting in the kitchen watching her as she baked her annual batch of Christmas cookies, she would have accused that person of heavily dipping into the eggnog. In fact, perhaps she could use a nip of something like eggnog herself. Maybe something stronger.

Why was she so jittery? Her sugar cookie recipe called for precision and care, or the dough turned too sticky and was impossible to work with. She didn't have time for that kind of complication. Her nerves seemed to not want to cooperate. There was no excuse for it. After all, she'd had an audience while baking in the past. Myrna had always kept her company in the kitchen during this annual tradition.

Granted, Zayn was most definitely not Myrna.

Izzy stole a glance at him now as he pulled out one of the wooden stools and sat at the counter. The collar of his white dress shirt was undone, exposing just a triangle of toned skin; again that wayward dark curl fell over his forehead above his eye. The man had taken a spill and gotten hurt less than an hour ago. How did he still manage to look so sexy and attractive? He'd rolled up his sleeves and she couldn't help but notice the muscular contours of his arms. An unbidden image of the last time those arms were around her waist sprang into her mind.

She gave a shake to her head. Thoughts such as those were not going to do anything to steady her nerves.

"Can I help in any way?" he asked from his perched position. "Not that I've baked anything in the recent past."

She quirked an eyebrow at him. "Or ever?"

"Or ever."

She grabbed an apron where it hung on the wall by the sink, put it over her head and tied the straps behind her back. "You can definitely help me cut out the dough later. This first part is all me, I'm afraid."

"Sounds serious."

She nodded solemnly. "You can't take any chances with sugar cookie dough. Only a true expert can be trusted to craft its creation."

"Then I promise not to get in your way, Master Dough Expert."

She chuckled. "Thank you. But start summoning your creative side. You'll need it for the cutting out part."

"Not like I have anything else I can do." He didn't sound happy about it. No doubt he hated this development. Having to spend time sitting here in his aunt's old kitchen. This scene was much too bland for him, much too domesticated. She knew from tabloids and papers—not that she sought them out, but he was featured just often enough as to be unavoidable—that the life he led now was much more worldly.

Those arms she'd been admiring earlier had been around some of the most attractive women in the world, from models to actresses to rock stars. Yep, Zayn Joffman had done quite well for himself since leaving town. He'd achieved professional success at a level most people could only dream of. He had wealth, no small amount of fame, and a fantasy lifestyle. And all he'd had to do was leave his old life behind. Including her.

"And where did you just drift off to?" he asked from across the counter. She realized she'd been staring off into space for a considerable amount of time.

Pull it together.

"Just mentally recalling the recipe." She turned to the pantry to retrieve the pastry flour, powdered sugar and the rest of the dry ingredients.

Measuring out the various amounts, she stole another glance at Zayn. He was fidgeting to the point of barely sitting on the stool. The poor man really wasn't used to sitting still. Izzy could tell he was going stir-crazy. She had to give him something to do.

Why had she thought he could just sit there and do nothing? She knew him better than that.

"Actually, there is something you can do right now. Please grab the cookie cutters and give them a rinse. They've been sitting in the cupboard since last year."

He looked relieved. "Sure thing. Where are they?"

She pointed to a cupboard on the other side of the kitchen. "Take your time, though. You still need to be careful with that head wound."

He turned to her. "You don't really need my help here, do you? You just remembered what a nuisance I am when I have pent-up energy."

He'd caught her. "Busted. I know things can go badly when you're standing still."

She hadn't meant to say it that way. Zayn stilled in the process of shutting the cupboard door. His reaction told her the words had landed exactly as she hadn't wanted them to.

"Those days are past me, Izzy. You have to know that."

"Zayn, that's not what I intended at all. The words were wrong."

"I haven't so much as had a traffic violation in the past five years." His eyes rested heavy on her face.

"Not even a speeding ticket?" She said it jokingly to try to lighten the suddenly heavy mood between them. It didn't work.

"I'm not that kid anymore."

Izzy set the measuring cup down with a sigh. "Neither of us is exactly a kid now. We're not the same people."

He raised an eyebrow. "You know what I mean. I'm not the angry, confused kid I once was. The one always ready for a fight, physical or otherwise. The one who stayed out too late and fought against all the rules."

"I'm well aware of that." How could she not be? Look how far he'd come, with virtually no help from anyone else. His success was solely a result of his hard work, determination and sheer will. But he was wrong about the fighter part. That was the reason he had been able to achieve all that he had. Zayn had always been a fighter when it came to what he wanted.

He hadn't wanted *her*. Izzy forced away the

sharp pain that landed in the vicinity of her heart at the thought.

He studied her face before continuing. "Besides, you seem like your usual previous self."

Yow. Now it was her turn to be somewhat offended. "What's that supposed to mean?"

"Nothing derogatory. You're still a hard worker, loyal, with a large, loving family who adores you."

Izzy's spine stiffened. He was so wrong about that last part. So much had happened since he'd left. It would take too much emotional effort to explain all of it to him.

And this wasn't the time. So why did she want so badly to confide in him? He was the one man who'd torn her heart to shreds and left her without a backward glance. Without so much as an explanation as to his motives. She'd deserved at least an explanation.

But before all that, he'd been a close confidant. A friend. Someone she could turn to. A shoulder to cry on, an ear to bend. She'd missed having that. Especially this past year when everything had gone down between her and her father. She could have used a good friend to lean on during that time. More than a lover, she simply could have used someone to turn to.

Truth be told, when it came to Zayn Joffman, she missed so much more.

He would have known to simply listen, without trying to tell her what to do about disappointing Papa the way she had. He would have simply held her and soothed her when she'd explained that the choice she'd made was best for all involved. She'd chosen to continue working for Myrna rather than join her father's new winery because her and Papa were too alike, too intractable, and they would have butted heads constantly. She'd had no doubt her working for the family business would have resulted in permanent, irreparable damage to her relationship with her father.

Additionally, Papa had had her brother, numerous cousins, and Mama to help him get his winery up and running. Myrna had had no one. Not with Zayn gone.

Their respective pasts were the proverbial elephant in the room. So far, they'd been tiptoeing around it, but it would be naïve to think they could avoid confronting it altogether.

Zayn walked around the kitchen island and behind Izzy to the sink. The comfortable camaraderie they'd been enjoying just moments ago had evaporated like the top layer of wine in a barrel.

He turned on the water and held the various cookie cutters under the stream, one by one.

He'd often thought of this moment, what exactly he would say to her. Saying sorry seemed wholly inadequate. And, technically, he'd already done that years ago. Though back then, the timing had been way off. It seemed timing had been the root of all their problems so often in the past.

He grabbed the folded towel sitting on the counter next to the sink and went back to his stool to dry the cutters. The frowning expression on Izzy's face made him wince as he sat. She noticed.

"What's the matter? Does your head hurt?"

"No. I feel fine." He did physically, anyway.

There had to be a way to resume the easy flow of conversation. "So, will Christmas dinner be the usual boisterous, extravagant affair at the Veracruz house? With enough food and drink to feed a neighborhood?"

She didn't look up at him as she answered. "Always is. What about you? What are your plans for Christmas?"

Funny. It sounded, for all intents and purposes, like she was trying to change the subject. She clearly looked uncomfortable. But why would discussing her plans for the holidays with her family be a source of discomfort?

"I'll just be getting back from the Food and Wine Expo in Paris. So probably just a low-key couple of days at home to try to unwind." No need to elaborate on the rest of it. He didn't have to tell her that his dinner would consist of a catered meal for one, delivered from the bistro housed on the bottom floor of his Manhattan apartment building. Or how he'd probably just study spreadsheets, sitting alone on his sofa, a cheesy movie playing on his wide-screen TV until he fell asleep.

Same as it always had been.

"Sounds exciting." Again, her words were delivered tightly, flatly.

Curious. He got the impression there were things she wasn't saying, as well. So both of them were keeping secrets.

An hour later, when the dough was ready, they'd managed to avoid discussing anything of any substance whatsoever. Izzy washed her hands and dried them off. "That needs to chill. Let's get started on the frosting, then." She pointed to the plastic bag on the counter she'd pulled out earlier. "Pass me the powdered sugar, would you?"

Zayn shifted and pushed the bag over to her. Unfortunately, what he hadn't realized until that moment was that the bag had been opened already. A cloud of white powder erupted from the top and spread through the air.

"Uh-oh."

Izzy clasped a hand to her mouth. Through the cloud of white dust, she looked like a vision in some kind of late-night dream. Then she sneezed. And sneezed twice more.

He couldn't help himself. The sheer ridiculousness of the moment made him chuckle.

"Oh, you think that's funny, huh?" Izzy's voice held a hint of mischief that immediately had him on guard.

He was right. But he wasn't fast enough. In the next instant, she'd grabbed a handful of the sugar and flung it in his direction. It landed on his face, in his hair, all over him.

Now Izzy was laughing with abandon.

He made an elaborate show of brushing powder off his left shoulder. An utterly useless action, there was simply too much of it. Izzy laughed harder.

"Did you honestly think you were going to get away with that?"

Heeding the warning in his voice, she turned on her heel to get away. But the only exit from the kitchen was to pass by him. He didn't let her. Grabbing her from behind as she tried to run past the counter, he grabbed a small amount of the sugar and flung it in the air above them both. In a matter of seconds, they resembled eerie ghosts straight out of one of those old-fashioned black-and-white horror movies. Like the first film version of Scrooge.

Still, he didn't let her go. His arms tightened their hold of their own volition, her back snug against his chest. The smell of her hair tickled his nose, the fruity shampoo now mixed with the sweet scent of sugar. He was oh so tempted to run his tongue along the back of her neck, to taste her skin and breathe in her scent. Somehow, he resisted, though he thought he might die from the strain and the effort.

They both stopped laughing. The moment hung heavy between them; neither one moved for several beats. Finally, all too soon, Izzy pulled out of his embrace and stepped away. Then she turned to face him.

She looked utterly adorable, good enough to kiss. And lick.

He clenched his fists to keep from pulling her back into his embrace. It wasn't easy.

It took forever for all the dust to settle. When it finally did, the entire kitchen looked like a sugar bomb had exploded in the center. They both stood staring at the collateral damage.

"What a mess." He stated the obvious.

Izzy agreed with a nod and a sigh. "This will take forever to clean up."

She wasn't wrong. "Guess we'd better get started."

She went to grab the vacuum and Zayn took the moment to try to forget the way it had felt to hold her once again. His arms still tingled with the warm current of her skin against his.

A warmth that didn't diminish in all the time it took them to vacuum and mop the mess they'd had so much fun making together.

What had just happened?

Izzy tried hard to ignore the pounding in her chest. Her body felt aflame from head to toe after being in Zayn's arms. She'd set out to bake some Christmas cookies while she kept an eye on Zayn, like Ethan had instructed.

Somehow, she'd ended up pressed against him, her back tight against the length of his body. His breath tickling the back of her neck. She'd been oh so tempted to simply turn her head. His lips would no doubt have been close enough to touch hers if she'd done just that. Then who knew where things may have led. She shuddered at the thought.

Her life was messy enough right now. She didn't need the added complication of falling again for the ex that had left her without a thought, alone and desperately longing for him. That longing had resurfaced much too easily. She knew he'd felt it, too. There was no doubt they were still attracted to each other. He'd hardly been in town for a couple of days and she'd fallen into his arms not once but twice already.

No more. It couldn't happen again. Her heart couldn't take it.

"Uh, we should probably go get cleaned up," she ventured, not quite meeting Zayn's eyes. She was too afraid of what she'd see in their depths. So help her, if he showed any signs that he wanted her as much as she wanted him, she'd be tempted all over again.

What a fool she was.

"I guess I could use a shower," he answered.

A nagging thought struck her. She was supposed to be keeping a steady watch on him. Could she even leave him alone to shower? What if he got dizzy? Or lost his balance?

"I don't know about you showering alone, Zayn."

She wanted to kick herself for the way the words had just come out of her mouth.

The corners of Zayn's lips lifted. "Oh? Are you suggesting we shower together, then?"

Her mouth went dry at the thought. The two of them, under a hot and steamy spray, squeezed tight against each other in the stall. She shook the image off. "That's not what I meant and you know it."

He slowly shook his head. "What a shame, then. It would have conserved water."

"I commend your sudden concern for environmental issues. What about your head? What exactly is the concussion protocol when it comes to showers?"

He shrugged. "Damned if I know."

"We probably shouldn't risk it."

He gestured to his upper body. "I can't stay covered in powdered sugar."

"I know that!"

"Well, I'm out of ideas."

There was only one way she could think of. And it was going to be torture. "I'll stand outside the door while you shower."

The grin that appeared on his face was downright wolfish. "Yeah? You want to supervise?"

"Stop, Zayn. This isn't funny. I'm just trying to be responsible here." She should have asked Ethan to be more specific with his instructions.

"Sorry," he answered. "Between the painkillers and the goose egg, I'm saying things I probably shouldn't say."

Izzy's breath hitched. He probably shouldn't have said that bit, either. The moment was getting much too heated for comfort. "I just don't want you to get hurt again."

He crossed his arms in front of his chest.

"Huh. One might venture to guess that you're worried about my well-being."

"One would be mistaken. I simply don't want blood on my hands. Or on your head, for that matter."

"Because you care about me?"

"Let's just say it would put a damper on the festivities for our light display opening night if you took another spill."

In a move that sent a shiver down her spine, he reached over and tapped a finger to her nose. Then he licked the sugar off his finger. "If you say so, Iz."

He'd used her shortened name again. This time, she didn't have the wherewithal to protest. Instead, she gently took him by the elbow. "Let's go. The sooner you get in and out of the shower, the sooner I can take a long, relaxing one myself."

"I must repeat myself. It's a pity you won't entertain the idea of taking one together."

She ignored that as they made their way upstairs to his suite of rooms. Zayn grabbed a towel from the linen closet and went in to take his shower. Izzy sat on the edge of the bed, cursing herself for not having thought to bring a book or a magazine. Anything to occupy her brain. For the only thing she could think of right now was how Zayn was only a few feet away. Without any clothes on.

With a huff, she shot up off the bed and paced around the room. He really hadn't brought much with him. His laptop sat open on the antique wooden desk; several file folders lay strewed about the bed. He hadn't yet emptied his suitcase.

Clearly, he didn't plan on staying long. For all she knew, he would have been out of here already if she'd only agreed to sell and signed his blasted paperwork.

The recollection of the real reason he was there was like a splash of cold water down her back. What was she thinking? Relishing being in his arms. Laughing with him as they played food fight with powdered sugar. Bantering with him as he teased her about showering together. The man was essentially here for a business deal. One that meant to oust her out of the winery she considered home.

Right now, it was the only true home she had.

His cell phone suddenly lit up and vibrated on the desk with an incoming call. She stole a glance at the display. The contact info of the caller had her doing a double take. Lovely Clara.

Izzy felt her hands clench at her sides. Whoever this Clara was, she apparently warranted an affectionate misnomer. Who would have thought Zayn had turned into the type of man who entered endearing nicknames into the contact list of his phone? Then again, she didn't really know this new Zayn, did she? Perhaps she'd never known the man at all.

The sound of running water shut off and she stepped away from the desk as if caught in a clandestine, sneaky act. A minute after, the cell phone dinged the signal of a voice message.

"Lovely Clara" had certainly left a long-winded voice mail. Probably full of kissy noises and telling him she missed him and yearned for him to come back already.

As if Izzy needed yet another reminder that she had no business being attracted to Zayn Joffman in any way. Those days were long over.

The smell of vanilla and cinnamon gently roused him awake the next morning. Certainly it beat the stale, dry scent he woke up to in his own apartment most mornings. Or the standard bland air of an overscrubbed room in a high-rise hotel. The aroma was mouthwatering by comparison.

Zayn rolled over onto his back and slowly opened his eyes. The ache behind his forehead was there just enough to make itself known. Not wanting to take any chances to exacerbate it, he took his time sitting up.

The scent continued to beckon him. His nostrils registered the additional subtle aroma of fresh-brewed coffee.

Izzy must have made her usual strong Hawaiian roast and started on the cookies. Perhaps she'd been baking all night, for all he knew. He'd stepped out of his shower to be greeted by disappointment when he'd walked back into the room last night to find she'd left.

Then he'd finally fallen asleep after waiting with futile hope that perhaps she might return. Simply so that they could talk some more.

She hadn't.

The neon-green digital clock on his bedside table read 8:00 a.m. He couldn't recall the last time he'd slept in so late. Or so restfully. Maybe a good and solid hit to the old noggin did that to a guy. He threw on a T-shirt and the pair of sweats he'd packed and made his way downstairs.

He had to pause in the kitchen doorway to take a breath when he saw her.

Izzy had pulled her hair back into a high ponytail with a headband at the crown of her head to catch any wayward strands. She wore sweats herself, the leg cuffs rolled up to right below her knees. On her feet were the thickest socks he'd ever seen. The tank she had on hugged her in all the right places.

How did a woman look so sexy wearing fuzzy, thick socks, ratty sweats and a plain red tank top?

Zayn swallowed and stepped into the room, making sure not to stare. It wasn't at all easy.

"You're awake," she said just as a timer beeped loudly behind her. Grabbing a comically large oven mitt, she pulled a tray of fresh-baked cookies out of the oven. Several more trays sat on cooling racks strewed across various surfaces of the kitchen.

"I am. And apparently you've been awake for quite a while yourself."

She nodded. "I wanted to get a head start." She pointed to the coffee maker on the breakfast island in the corner by the pantry. "Just brewed another pot. Help yourself. The mugs are where they've always been."

"You've certainly gotten a head start, all right." He grabbed one of the larger mugs—stein-size—and poured himself a generous cup. "How long have you been up?"

"Since dawn," she answered. "Didn't have time to spare. We never did get around to making the frosting last night."

He'd forgotten that part. Amusement bubbled in his chest when he thought of the reason they had been waylaid. The sensation turned to heat when he thought about what had happened after.

The shower he'd taken last night, knowing she was only a few feet away, had been one of the most testing experiences of his life.

"Sorry, I wasn't much help."

"Don't worry about it. How do you feel?" she asked him, pulling off another hunk of dough from the massive ball that sat in a big silver bowl in the middle of her workspace.

"Fine. I had a great nursemaid taking care of me. I owe you one."

She shrugged. "I figured letting you get a good night's sleep was the best thing I could do for you after the day you'd had. Though I did check on you a couple times during the night. You were sleeping soundly and seemed to be shifting position." Her tone was very matter-of-fact.

She was different this morning. Distant. Fully focused on the task at hand. Zayn felt like an intrusive pest who was hindering her progress and distracting her needlessly.

"I see. Thanks." *I guess*, he added silently. If he were being honest, he'd have told her he would have preferred some company after the day he'd had. Her company.

Maybe he should have just come clean last night and told her so. He could have blamed it on the moment of levity they'd shared, the moment some of the ice between them had cracked.

He could have even conveniently used the head injury as an excuse. For one brief moment, he'd had an opportunity to ask her to stay with him. Simply to talk. To catch up on each other's lives. He'd blown it by missing the opportunity to do so.

It occurred to him he may never get another chance.

CHAPTER SEVEN

IZZY WANTED TO forget all her concerns and troubles and all the questions plaguing her about Zayn and his reasons for being at Stackhouse. She just wanted to enjoy the evening. This night always brought out her holiday cheer, though it was all rather bittersweet this year with Myrna gone. She just knew her mentor was there in spirit. Izzy would like to think she'd be impressed. She'd worked hard to get everything just right.

Tomorrow morning, she would return to worrying about what she was going to do about Zayn, or the mess that was currently her family life. Tonight she just wanted to enjoy the fruits of her labor.

The day spent baking and cleaning and setting up had given her time to think and come to her senses. Zayn might be visiting right now, but he was no longer a fixture in her life. He was only planning to stay for a few more days. And once they resolved the whole issue of ownership, she most likely would hardly hear from him. She had to move on, go forward with her life, just as he clearly had done with Lovely Clara.

She wondered if he'd even bother to come out and join in the festivities. He didn't seem at all interested and she knew he disagreed with the concept overall. And he probably still had a headache.

Izzy took a deep breath and pushed the useless thoughts away. Tonight was about tonight.

A familiar voice shouted out from behind her, "There's my beautiful, talented sister."

A smile immediately found her lips. "Hey, Hector. You're back in town."

He wrapped her in a bear hug, as was his customary greeting when he saw her these days. Izzy knew he was trying to compensate and she appreciated it. Still, it just made things all the more awkward. Poor Hector was just caught in the middle of the drama between her and her father. She knew Papa loved her. He just had a funny way of showing it.

"Got in this afternoon. Took an earlier flight just so I wouldn't miss all this." He looked around appreciatively. "You did a great job."

He landed a small, affectionate peck on her cheek. "I'm gonna go fix myself a plate. I'm starving."

She had to laugh. Hector was always starving. At a little over six feet, with the general frame of a bean pole, she had no idea where he put it all. Whereas all her calories seemed to land in the general vicinity of her hips. They'd definitely inherited a different set of genes from their parents.

"Help yourself," she told him. "I'm sure I'll see you around later at some point."

As her brother walked away, she found herself scanning the rapidly growing crowd. All the regulars were already here. Mr. Reyes, his wife and two of their grandchildren mingled in the smaller tent across the pathway. Izzy spotted Ethan and Paula standing over by the vines. They appeared to be in the middle of what had to be a depthless, innocuous conversation. She knew they were both insanely attracted to each other but were too shy to do anything about it.

No sign of Zayn. Not that she'd been specifically looking for him.

The swell of disappointment in her chest made her a hopeless fool. There was no reason to think Zayn would attend. And absolutely no reason for her to want him to so badly.

Zayn supposed there were worse ways to spend the evening. Izzy's light display opening night was like one big outdoor party. He found himself being pulled into the spirit of it all, despite his general disdain for the entire affair. Maybe Izzy was right. Maybe he was simply being a Grinch. Or a money-focused businessman the likes of Ebenezer Scrooge himself.

In his defense, he was only thinking about the bottom line. And he just didn't see what all this did to contribute to that end. Still, he could see why Izzy and Myrna had enjoyed the tradition so much.

Outdoor speakers set up around the grounds and along the perimeter of the vines filled the air with bouncy Christmas music. A mountain of cookies sat piled on a center table already loaded with other munchies and snacks. Wine was being poured generously in every corner and several large thermos pumps had been set up to dispense hot chocolate to those underage.

All in all, he was impressed. Izzy had put all this together, mostly herself. Not that he should be surprised. She'd always been a study in efficiency and competence. And she managed to do it all with grace and style.

She approached him, dressed in a festive red-and-green wrap dress, a pointy Santa hat flopped over her head. Lace-up red boots with springy pom-poms on the laces rounded out the outfit. She looked like a fetching, sexy Mrs. Claus. Santa should be so lucky.

People were slowly starting to trickle in. Izzy had told him earlier that she'd planned to flip the switch and turn every display on in about an hour or so, just as the sky turned dark.

"I'm glad you decided to join us," she said with a smile, speaking loudly over the music—some lively Latin version of "Jingle Bells."

"I managed to summon some holiday cheer, after all." That was partially true. The fact was he'd spent the day working and had found himself counting down the minutes until he had an excuse to come out here to see her again.

"It's a Christmas miracle." She nudged him with her shoulder playfully. The warmth and good humor of last night was back. He was glad for it. Though it probably had less to do with him than the fact that Izzy was in her element right now. She'd worked hard to make this night a success and she'd done a great job. They already had a good number of visitors even though it was still rather early.

How she managed to look so fresh and energetic after working all day to put this together, he couldn't begin to guess.

The smile grew wider. "You've gone quiet. What are you thinking?"

"I'm thinking you're pretty darn miraculous yourself."

Her eyes flashed with surprise. He hadn't meant to say that; she'd caught him off guard.

"Oh?"

He gave what he hoped was an unaffected smile. First, he'd shamelessly joked about showering together last night—he should probably find a way to apologize for that. And now he was throwing unguarded compliments her way. As if they were a couple again.

"I just mean to say it's pretty incredible what you've managed to put together out here. I'm impressed."

She wiggled her eyebrows at him. "Even though you don't agree with the general idea?"

He stifled a groan. "Let's not get into all that right now. Just take the compliment, why don't you?"

"I will, then," she answered with a small bow. "So, thank you. For the compliment."

"You're welcome... I could have come down and helped you. You only needed to ask." It stung a bit that she hadn't.

"I had it under control. Besides, you don't do well being bossed around."

She had a point there. "Never did well with authority, did I? As the local sheriff's office can attest."

He'd had so much anger back in those days, such a chip on his shoulder. It's why he'd agreed to get out of town before he destroyed himself, as well as everyone in his general orbit. Including his great-aunt. And Izzy.

"If those cops could see you now. A self-made international success story."

Her words served to send a flush of pleasure through his system. Like he was a puppy and she'd just thrown him a chew treat.

"They'd probably find an excuse to arrest me again. Zayn the Troublemaker back in town," he retorted with a chuckle.

"Not like you didn't give them cause."

"Yeah, thankfully that's all behind me. These days, there'd be no one to bail me out." His aunt had given up on doing so after about the fourth or fifth time.

"Really? There isn't anyone?"

It sounded like a serious question. Somehow, he'd apparently lost the scope of the conversation. They were talking hypotheticals and joking around. Weren't they? So why was she staring at him so intently as she waited for an answer? She had to know he had no intention of doing anything that might land him in any kind of cell. He hadn't been in one for a long time.

"There has to be somebody," she persisted.

He gave a small shrug. Whatever this little wordplay game was, he supposed he'd go along with it. "I guess Clara might. She's my admin assistant."

She blinked up at him, confusion and some unknown emotion clouding her eyes. "You're dating your admin assistant?"

He nearly choked on the sip of wine he'd just taken. "What? Good God, no. Where'd you get that idea?"

She looked away, studied her fingertips. "I was just guessing."

"You've guessed so far wrong you've almost committed a crime yourself."

"I did?"

He turned to her then. "What's this about? Are you trying to ask me if I'm involved with someone, Iz?"

Her head flung up. "What? No! Of course not."

Right. That didn't sound convincing at all. Zayn found himself ridiculously pleased that she was inquiring about his personal life. Comically, she was doing a rather poor job of it. He decided to throw her a bone.

"I date occasionally." As she must know if she glanced at any kind of social media or business/entertainment website. "Very casual dating. Nothing has panned out into any kind of serious relationship. And I'm certainly not dating any of my employees." He shuddered at the thought and the potential complications of such behavior. "Clara Lovely happens to be my very efficient, very experienced assistant." The thought of him dating the nearly retired grandmother of five had him chuckling.

"I see. Well, I just assumed…" She paused suddenly. "Wait, what did you just say? She's lovely?"

"That's her name. Clara Lovely. Dutch. Or perhaps Swedish. I'm not quite sure."

She must have found the name incredibly funny for she bent over with laughter. There were times he didn't understand women at all. He certainly had trouble understanding this one more often than not.

In any case, two could play at this game. "What about you?" he asked once she'd straightened.

"Me?"

He nodded. "You must be seeing someone." His gaze landed on the edge of the line of vines where Ethan stood with Stackhouse's product manager, Paula. The blonde with the ponytail. "Doc Ethan seemed very eager to assist you with the display setup."

She snorted a laugh. "Trust me, that was not for my benefit."

"No?"

She shook her head with vehemence. "Not

at all." She lifted her chin in Ethan's direction. "He's mostly doing it out of the kindness of his heart. But also to impress and hang out near Paula. Those two have the hots for each other and have had for years. Neither one is doing anything about it, though. Who knows why?"

Zayn felt a sudden empathy and unexpected kinship with the charismatic doctor he'd been so annoyed with just a few seconds ago. He could relate to the poor soul. He would have to buy the man an ale at some point.

Izzy continued, her gaze focused on the ever-growing crowd. She wasn't meeting his eye. "I'm not involved with anyone. Certainly not Ethan."

The breath of relief Zayn released was audible. If Izzy noticed, she didn't comment on it.

He didn't get a chance to probe further as Izzy was approached by several newcomers. The crowd around them had grown considerably during the course of their conversation. Zayn watched her as she greeted her guests with characteristic warmth and friendliness. She really was something. He'd missed her. He had to admit that to himself once and for all.

If he was the sort to flatter himself, he might have even thought she'd been acting jealous when she'd asked about Clara earlier. Zayn took another sip of his wine, pleased beyond words at the overall direction the conversation had taken.

Izzy could feel Zayn's eyes on her two hours later as the celebrations were in full swing. She knew he'd been eyeing her for most of the night. When she thought about how foolish she'd been…assuming he was dating someone when the whole thing was a complete misunderstanding. Not that it was any of her business. Zayn Joffman could date anyone he pleased.

The lighting of the displays had gone off without a hitch and so far the night was a complete success. Ethan's electrician friend had come through and the weather was cooperating nicely. All in all, things were running along quite well. So why did it feel like her stomach was tied in knots? Every time she glanced up to find Zayn watching her, the knots grew a little tighter. This was right around the time of the night when she should be beginning to relax. Instead, she felt like a teenager at a school dance wondering if her crush had noticed her.

Snap out of it. You're a professional adult.

But her mind ignored the directive as she noticed Zayn was walking toward her.

"Now you've gone and done it," he told her, his voice loaded and serious.

What on earth was he referring to? "Done what?"

He pointed to a spot above her head. "You're standing under mistletoe."

She looked up to confirm he was indeed right. One of the beams along the ceiling of the tent had a dangling mistletoe plant right above where she stood. She had no idea who might have put it there. If she'd known, she might have taken care not to get caught under the darn thing. But here she was, right in the line of fire.

As if it was some sort of sign.

Her breath caught in her chest when she looked back at Zayn. His gaze was fixated squarely on her lips. His eyes had grown impossibly dark. Slowly, dreamily, he lowered his face to hers. Out of pure instinct, she bit down on her lower lip.

Heaven help her, she had no doubt what he was about to do. And she had no doubt that she wanted him to. Very much.

Her mind cried out that it would be all wrong. She shouldn't want this, couldn't want it. This was the man who had left her after breaking her heart. He was the one who'd replied with nonanswers when she'd emailed and called and texted to ask why. He was only here now because he wanted to oust her out of her very position as part owner of the winery she called home.

He'd be gone again in a matter of days.

What treacherous manner of heart did she have beating in her chest that she was ready to forget all that and long for him to kiss her?

She swallowed past the dryness that suddenly coated her tongue. "I have no idea how that got there. It's not part of the decorations."

"How lucky for me that it is." He leaned toward her then, reaching his arm behind her along her waist.

With the touch of his lips against hers, all the doubts and trepidation seemed to vanish into thin air. The crowd around them no longer existed. All that mattered was the taste of him, the warmth of skin against hers.

She felt as if time had reversed herself and she was catapulted back to the young woman she'd been all those years ago, being held and kissed by the only man she'd ever fallen in love with. The only one she'd loved since.

The moment was over all too soon. When he pulled away, she felt the loss like a physical ache. "We'll have to figure out who's responsible for the mistletoe," he whispered against her cheek, his breath hot on her skin. "So that I can properly thank them."

Before she could summon a response, she heard her brother's voice. "Zayn? Is that you, my man?"

Hector, she realized, clearly hadn't seen what had just transpired between the two of them.

Zayn immediately dropped his arm from around her middle and pulled away.

When her brother reached them, he and Zayn did some version of a complicated handshake before bumping shoulders. For an insane moment, Izzy felt a twinge of disappointment toward her only sibling. She'd always considered it somewhat disloyal that Hector still considered Zayn a close friend. That made absolutely no sense given she was her own person and so was Hector. He and Zayn had been close friends in high school and had played on the same baseball team. Not to mention, she'd been locking lips with Zayn only moments ago.

Suffice it to say, her feelings for her ex were rather complicated. Kissing him in a crowd of people certainly did not help matters.

"I heard you were back in town," her brother was saying.

"Not for long, I'm afraid," Zayn answered, once more dousing her with a good splash of reality. "Just here on some business." He gave Izzy a pointed look.

Business that involved her. Issues they were nowhere near resolving.

Hector stuck a finger out at him. "Let me tell you, bro. You could have done worse as a

business partner. I bet she didn't even tell you."
He turned to her. "Did you, Izzy? About the
award?"

Izzy drew a deep breath. She really didn't
need to get into that particular topic with Zayn.
There was no need.

"She didn't tell me anything about any
award," Zayn answered for her. He lifted an
inquisitive eyebrow. "Care to do so now?"

"There's really no need."

"Sure there is, sis," Hector argued. "One of
her cabernets from last year is up for an award
from the editors at *World Vintner* magazine.
She's just being her usual humble self."

Zayn studied her. "Is that so?"

"It's not a big deal. A French restaurateur who
was out here for a tasting submitted it as a nom-
inee upon returning to Paris. I highly doubt it
will win."

"You don't know that," Hector countered.
"She's not even going out there for the ceremony. Can you believe it?"

The eyebrow lifted even higher. "Why not?"

She shrugged her shoulder. "I hadn't really
thought about it. There's been quite a bit going
on, between the holidays, rounding out the end
of harvest season and…" She knew she didn't
need to say the rest out loud. Losing Myrna had
been an unexpected and heartbreaking shock.

The last thing on her mind had been some pretentious award everyone would forget about a year from now.

Her brother had other ideas about it, however. Ideas she had no intention of entertaining in Zayn's presence.

CHAPTER EIGHT

ZAYN WASN'T SURE if he was following the conversation fully. He felt a little loopy and it had nothing to do with the two glasses of wine he'd had—though that certainly wasn't helping matters. No, the real issue was what had just happened between him and Izzy. He was still experiencing the aftereffects of that mind-blowing kiss. Neither his body nor his soul had been prepared to taste her again. Now that he had, he knew he needed more. Whatever had happened between them up until now, however badly he'd messed up in the past, the spark they'd shared still burned as bright and powerful as it had ever had. He knew she'd felt it, too. How could she not?

He couldn't wait to taste her again, would have succumbed to the urge to retake her lips in his if it hadn't been for Hector. The arrival of her brother had thrown a proverbial bucket of cold water over the hottest of moments. Now the two siblings were arguing about some award Izzy was up for. Zayn had heard of it, of course. The magazine she'd referenced was well-known. She may not be terribly impressed with the accolade, but very well should have been. The honor she was up for was a fairly prestigious one.

"Come on, sis…" Hector was saying. "You know this might be a way to break through to him once and for all."

Who was this *him* they were talking about? Was it a high-end buyer? Or an industry influencer perhaps? It didn't sound like Hector was referring to any kind of romantic interest. Or maybe that was just wishful thinking on Zayn's part. Either way, it was just one more mystery.

Hector continued. "You know how much credence he gives to things like that."

Izzy laid a hand on his forearm. "I appreciate what you're trying to do, Hector. And I love you for it. I really do. But I don't want to talk about this right now. I just want to enjoy the evening and pour my first glass of wine. Things are finally at a point where I can relax and enjoy the night."

Hector looked ready to argue, but must have thought better of it. He deflated like a pricked balloon before speaking again. "Fine. But we're not done. This conversation isn't over. We can stop for now because you've earned a little rest and relaxation."

"Thank you."

"I'll go get you your wine," Hector said.

She patted him affectionately on the shoulder. "That's what a good sibling is for."

Hector didn't return her smile, merely rolled his eyes at her.

"Please don't ask," she said as her brother left them, giving Zayn the full-on side-eye. Right. Like he'd be able to help himself.

"I find that I must. What was that all about? Did I hear correctly that you're up for the *World Vintner*'s award in the cabernet category? That's a highly regarded magazine."

How had he not known about this? What he did know was that the ceremony was to be held during the Food and Wine Expo in Paris, precisely where he was headed next.

Izzy blew out a puff of air that lifted the bangs off her forehead. "Not a big deal. I was nominated for an award I have no interest in receiving."

"Why not?"

"Because it's not that important."

"I think it's pretty important. Clearly, Hector does, too."

"Yeah, well, his reasoning leaves a lot to be desired as far as I'm concerned."

"Reasons like prestige, attention, exposure? Sounds like pretty solid reasoning to me."

She didn't respond, just continued to study the crowd.

"Who was Hector referring to just now?"

She was silent so long, Zayn figured she wasn't going to answer at all. Finally, she spoke. "My father. We've been at odds. Hector thinks me being nominated might somehow break the stalemate between us."

"What kind of stalemate?"

Her body seemed to tense from head to toe and a slight sheen appeared in her eyes. When she answered, the hurt behind her words was as clear as the light surrounding them. "My father hasn't spoken to me in about thirteen months. Doesn't return my calls or pretends he hasn't received them. He makes himself scarce when I visit the house." Her voice quivered as she delivered the last word.

That didn't sound like Ernesto Veracruz at all. And it certainly didn't sound like the father who'd been so concerned about his daughter's future that he'd asked Zayn to leave town.

"Why would he—" Zayn didn't bother to finish asking the question as understanding began to dawn. Thirteen months. That was right around the time her family had officially opened their own winery. Aunt Myrna had mentioned that Ernesto hadn't been happy that Izzy had remained a Stackhouse employee rather than join her family in their endeavor. He hadn't realized her decision had caused such a rift.

Ernesto had always been so protective of his daughter, so proud of how smart she was, how hard she worked. And now they weren't even speaking. The reality of it seemed terribly wrong.

"I'm sorry, Izzy." He meant it, more than she might ever realize. "I have no doubt he'll eventually come around." He meant that, too. Everything he knew about Izzy and the man who was her father told Zayn this was a temporary bump in their relationship.

Still, there was no mistaking the toll the estrangement was having on Izzy. He wanted to ease her hurt, to help her soothe the pain. He knew firsthand the gaping wounds that came of absentee parents. It would be especially hard for Izzy. Her family had always been so close, with such a tight bond between them all. He'd been witness to their affection for each other through the years over countless dinners at the Veracruz house.

"He can't see why I chose to stay at Stackhouse," Izzy began, her voice low and strained. "I tried to explain that Myrna needed me more. She had no one really to help and she was at an age where she couldn't do as much. Paula hasn't been employed at Stackhouse very long… He's just being stubborn," she added after a pause.

Zayn didn't bother to point out that her father probably felt the same way about her.

"I find myself agreeing with your brother," he declared. "I think you should go to Paris. Not for Ernesto. Not to try to prove anything to him. But for yourself."

Izzy released a deep sigh. "The timing is just off, that's all. How can I drop everything here and go to Paris right now?"

"Why can't you? You said yourself that the season has wrapped up. Hector offered to help with the cleanup and maintenance. And I thought you said the barreling would only take another day or two."

"I just can't, Zayn. I haven't made any kind of plans to travel. The ceremony is in three days. I have no hotel, no itinerary, no plane ticket."

"Logistics," he told her, "which can easily be addressed. In fact, you can leave all that to me."

She scoffed at that. "Are you taking up travel agent as your next career?"

No, but an idea had begun to spark in his head and wouldn't stop niggling at him. It made no sense. Or it made all the sense in the world. He could just guess how Izzy would react when he told her. On the surface, his reasoning was solid. They were partners, they co-owned a winery and she was up for an award for that winery's cabernet. He'd made some spur-of-the-moment decisions in the past that had worked out pretty well for him.

None of this had anything whatsoever to do with that kiss.

"Come with me when I leave for Paris, Izzy."

Her eyes grew wide with astonishment. "What? Zayn, no."

"Why not? We could attend the expo together, make it to your ceremony, and maybe get up to speed on the latest trade developments."

"I don't…"

"Think about it," he urged at her pause. "You can hop onto my itinerary. We could do some sightseeing. At the least, we may even have a little fun."

Her tongue darted out to worry her bottom lip. "I'm going to stick to my original answer, Zayn. No."

Maybe he should have asked her after she'd had the glass of wine. The more he thought about it, the more it made sense for them to make the trip together. She couldn't just ignore the honor she'd been nominated for. What if she did in fact win and she wasn't even there to accept the trophy? And if it was in fact an opportunity to crack the tension between her and Ernesto, wasn't it worth taking?

He pressed further. "You still haven't given me a reason. Not any kind of real one."

"There are too many reasons to count. Our past history being one."

"We'd only be going as business partners. Nothing more. You have to agree we have a lot to discuss and negotiate. What better time and place to make decisions about our mutual winery than at the French wine expo during a year you happen to be up for an award?"

She shook her head, still not moved by his urging. It stung a little bit that she was so doggedly turning down an offer to travel with him, even as simply his business partner.

"You don't have to stay the whole week. I'll have my crew bring you back right after the ceremony, if that's what you wish."

She sucked in her bottom lip, deep in thought. Maybe he was getting to her finally.

Her next words had hope blossoming in his chest. "Let me sleep on it."

He could deal with that. That gave him all night to work on her. He could be very convincing when he wanted something badly enough.

And he hadn't wanted anything this badly in as long as he could remember.

* * *

He'd kissed her.

Close to twelve hours had gone by since it had happened and she could still feel the tingle on her lips. The taste of him still lingered on her tongue. Izzy turned up the hot water of the shower spray as far as she could without scalding her skin.

Damn the man. He'd had her tossing and turning all night. If she wasn't thinking about his lips on hers, she was recalling the heat she'd seen behind his eyes when he'd pointed out the mistletoe and leaned in to take her lips with his own.

She'd found out later that one of the hands who was aware of Paula's crush on Ethan had placed the plants strategically around the vineyard and grounds, hoping they would prompt one of the besotted yet shy lovebirds to finally make the first move.

Only, Izzy had been the one caught in the trap instead. And she truly did feel trapped.

Zayn wanted her to travel with him to Paris. Another thought that had kept her up all night. She couldn't seriously consider going, could she?

She really did feel indifferent about the award nomination. She didn't need a miniature statue to tell her worth as a vintner. Hector, on the other hand, thought it was a golden opportunity—in more ways than one. Her brother saw this nomination as a channel for a way for Izzy to get back into her father's good graces. But she wasn't so sure.

Ernesto Veracruz could be a very stubborn man, particularly when it came to his only daughter. The daughter who'd had the nerve to turn him down last year when he'd asked her to help manage the winery her family had established. In many ways, given where he came from, her father had viewed her refusal as a rejection and sign of disrespect. Nothing could have been further from the truth. Izzy had more respect for her parents and all they'd accomplished than they would ever guess.

Papa had asked her to make an impossible decision—to choose between loyalty to him and *family* versus Stackhouse Winery and Myrna.

Grabbing the lavender body wash from the stall shelf, she lathered her bath sponge and inhaled deeply of the soothing, calming scent. She owed Zayn an answer today. Technically her answer should be obvious. She knew exactly what she should do: turn him down with the clear understanding that the subject was closed.

So why was she stalling in the shower? This was the third time she'd sponged herself down. At this rate, she was going to run out of hot water and emerge wrinkled and shivering. She had no business traveling anywhere with the likes of Zayn Joffman.

The question had to be asked. Would she even be considering his offer if it hadn't been for that kiss? She had to have been oblivious to not have noticed the mistletoe plants around the property. Almost comical, really. Someone had been trying to nudge Ethan and Paula along but had ended up forcing her hand instead.

If only those two could finally confront their feelings for each other once and for all. Izzy stilled in the act of scrubbing her shoulder. Of all the hypocritical takes. She was one to talk. She should have done some confronting herself. The moment Zayn had kissed her last night, she should have demanded some answers. A man didn't kiss a woman like that unless he was affected, too. The heat that she'd seen swimming behind his eyes bespoke an attraction that he'd be hard pressed to deny if pushed. It was high time she got some answers.

He owed it to her to tell her why he'd fled five years ago. And the answers had to be better than the unsatisfactory ones he'd been giving so far. He'd been committed to her and then he'd simply left. Judging from his behavior and the way they'd fallen into each other's arms within hours of him coming back was proof that neither one of them had gotten over each other. He was the one who had to explain why he'd felt the need to end it.

But she couldn't go at him with guns blazing. That hadn't worked five years ago, had only driven him further and further away. Maybe they did need to spend some time together. Maybe they needed to be somewhere far away from where the past had all gone down.

Or maybe her mind was simply making excuses for where her heart wanted to lead.

CHAPTER NINE

HAD HE DONE the right thing?

Zayn had the same thought that had plagued him for the past several hours as he escorted Izzy into the waiting limo after their flight landed.

It had seemed like such a good idea at the time, offering to have Izzy join him on this trip. As thrilled as he was that she'd agreed, he couldn't help now but wonder if he'd been caught up in the moment, in the headiness of that kiss they'd shared. Surrounded by jazzy music during a balmy evening with couples dancing all around them and wine flowing freely, he'd hadn't even questioned his instincts.

But reality was now staring him right in the face. He had three full days with Izzy in one of the most romantic cities in the world.

An awkward silence hung in the air between them as the driver eased into traffic to take them to the hotel. Izzy had slept for most of the flight, fallen asleep right after takeoff. He'd always envied that about her. The woman could sleep through anything, even turbulent jet flights.

So inviting her along on this trip had been something of an impulsive, spur-of-the-moment decision. Though not a conscious thought at the time, Zayn realized now that he'd been dreading yet another European visit by himself. Being here alone, particularly around the holidays, had always left him with a cold, hollow emptiness. So he'd been selfish, pretending the invite was a favor to Izzy when, at least on some level, he'd only been thinking of himself. Some things never changed.

Izzy hadn't been too far off track when she'd called him selfish his first day back in Napa.

"This is stunning," Izzy said across the seat from him. She had her forehead pressed against the glass of the car window. "I didn't realize how lovely Paris was during the Christmas season."

Outside, the city was decorated to within an inch of itself—festive mini Christmas trees, wreaths on light poles, and brightly colored window displays.

This! She was proving him right. This was why he had wanted her here. He wouldn't have even bothered to take the time to notice sidewalk decorations, choosing rather to focus on answering emails or updating project spreadsheets.

"Wait till you see it at night," he told her. "The Champs-Élysées has a spectacular light display." He gave her a teasing smile. "It might even compete with the one you put forth yourself at Stackhouse."

"I'd love to see that," she answered, not looking away from the scenery as they drove down the city streets.

"We can head there tonight if you're up for it. Gets chilly, though. Mild compared to the US east coast but still rather frosty. I hope you brought some outerwear."

"A few sweaters," she replied. "I don't really have anything winter worthy, living in Napa."

That wouldn't do. He would have to see about keeping her warm. That thought brought forth mental images he had no business thinking given that they were here on…well, business.

"Maybe we can visit some of the shops. They do a rather excellent job of Christmas window displays. Or we could visit one of the Christmas markets that are put up around the city this time of year." That was a much safer idea than what had run through his mind earlier.

Izzy turned to face him then and the smile on her face sent a surge of pleasure through his core. "That sounds lovely, Zayn. I've never been to a Christmas market in Europe. I can't wait to experience it."

Surprisingly, neither could he. He wouldn't have even entertained visiting the shops or markets during the busy Christmas season. But with Izzy here, the concept held a distinct appeal.

About half an hour later, he helped her out of the car once they got to their destination. A bellhop immediately appeared to handle their luggage while Zayn led her through the front door so that they could check in.

Izzy gasped in pleasure when they stepped inside the hotel. The lobby looked like the North Pole had exploded on the first floor of one of Paris's deluxe luxury hotels. An immensely tall, white-pine Christmas tree reached the high ceiling, fake presents with large red bows surrounding its base. By the entrance, eight reindeer statues were strapped to a wood sleigh that held a smiling mechanical Santa whose hand waved to and fro.

Had this hotel always done such an elaborate setup for the holidays? He probably hadn't even noticed. Now that he was seeing it all through Izzy's eyes, he felt like a child on Christmas morning. Any other child perhaps; his own childhood hadn't held many happy memories of the holidays. Or none at all, to be more accurate.

"Oh, my!" Izzy exclaimed, pausing next to

him to admire the distinctively French-looking Santa. He was actually wearing a bright red beret and his short beard resembled more of a white goatee. Zayn had to chuckle. "Let's get to checking in, shall we?"

Izzy nodded and followed him to the front desk. Where they were immediately met with a snafu.

"Your room is all ready, *monsieur*. The bell-man will take you right up," the attendant announced in perfect English with a heavy French accent.

"You mean room*s*?" Zayn corrected. "There are two of us traveling. The arrangements should have been made two days ago."

The man's brow furrowed as his perfectly manicured fingers flew across his computer keyboard. "I'm afraid there is only the one room under your name, sir."

That didn't make any sense. Clara had to have registered Izzy under her own room. "Try Izadora Veracruz."

The man shook his head. "I'm afraid there is nothing here for that individual, either."

Izzy stiffened next to him. "There must be some kind of mistake."

"My administrative assistant would have called to make an additional reservation. Could you recheck the spelling?"

The attendant did so, only to look back up at him worriedly. "I have nothing but the one room in your name, sir. Perhaps there was a language issue."

Zayn rubbed his chin. This didn't bode well. "Perhaps. May we simply add an additional room to the reservation, then?"

The man audibly scoffed. "We have been booked months in advance due to the expo, sir. I'm afraid there is nothing available. I'd be happy to give you each a separate key."

Izzy stepped over to the desk, her face ashen. "But it's not like that. We…aren't…you know… we aren't together or anything."

Izzy most definitely did not want to share a room with him. Not that he could really blame her under the circumstances. Still, his ego took a bit of a bruising at her reaction.

She turned to him, mild panic in her eyes. "Maybe another hotel nearby."

The attendant shot that idea down before Zayn could answer in kind. "The entire city is at capacity. You are welcome to call around, however."

Zayn took her gently by the elbow and pulled her aside. "These are very large suites, Izzy. I'll just sleep on the couch. We'll only have to share a bathroom. Like roomies. It will be fine."

She hardly looked convinced.

* * *

Well, this was a mistake. An unmitigated, full-blown disaster of a mistake. Izzy stepped into the hotel room behind Zayn and took in the luxurious surroundings as she stood in the doorway.

The place looked like something right out of a romantic movie, exactly what a honeymoon suite would look like. They did say Paris was the city for lovers. Obviously, the hotel industry took that reputation to heart when choosing their décor.

Plush, thick carpeting the color of desert sand, with gold-tone paint on the walls. Subtle hues of deep burgundy and rose-pink adorned the bed and furniture. A huge painting of a cherub hung on the wall above the wide-screen television.

Honestly, it all bordered on cliché, complete with the Eiffel Tower in view outside a glass door that led to a charming balcony.

This is what she got for ignoring her instincts and blindly following her impulsive heart. How in the world was she going to spend the next few days sharing this space with Zayn, her ex-lover?

"It won't be so bad," he said from across the room, as if reading her thoughts. "There's plenty of space. I promise I'll be a perfect gentleman."

Ha! As if she'd believe that. "Unless I happen to come to stand under some mistletoe?"

The smile he gave her was downright wolf-ish. "Well, I'm not made of stone."

She chose to ignore that. His eyes fell to the sofa in the center of the room just as hers did. The problem was immediately obvious. Far from any kind of comfortable place to sleep, the piece looked like it would barely fit a man of Zayn's stature. Given its size, the ornate armrests and a curved cushioned back would no doubt have him rolling off onto the floor in the middle of the night.

"I'll sleep on the sofa," she declared, stating what was clearly the only option.

Zayn grabbed his luggage and began unpacking. "You can't seriously think I'll allow that."

Why had she hoped he would just accept her wishes? Honestly, it was as if she didn't know him at all. "And I can't allow you to try to contort yourself into a pretzel shape in the very hotel room you booked and are paying for."

"You'll have to. Like I said, I am a true gentleman. One who would never let a lady spend a night on—" he pointed to the sofa in question "—that thing."

"Then we are clearly at an impasse."

He shrugged. "Let's discuss it over dinner. I'm famished."

Another thing they were going to put off addressing until later. But her stomach grumbled in response to the mention of food, so she decided not to push it. "I insist that it be my treat. You're paying for the hotel room. I'll pay for the meals." Only as the words left her mouth did she begin to question them. Knowing Zayn, he was probably used to eating in the finest, top-star restaurants. A place like that would probably cost her a pretty penny. She lived a comfortable life, but she was trying to stick to a budget. The winery always needed some equipment repair or upkeep and she desperately wanted to renovate the tasting room.

"It's a deal," Zayn agreed, surprising her by not arguing.

Looked like she would have to budget harder when she got back to California.

When they made it outside, the air had definitely grown chillier. A frosty breeze bit at her and she shivered in the too thin sweater. Zayn noticed. He shrugged off his scarf and handed it to her.

"Thanks. You weren't kidding about the nip in the air."

Inhaling deeply as she wrapped the scarf around her shoulders, she sank into its warmth. The scent of him filled her nostrils—sandalwood combined with a hint of lemon citrus and a distinctive tinge that was purely male and purely Zayn.

The scent flooded her senses, reminding her of the times he'd sneaked into her bedroom in the middle of the night and left his scent behind when he'd sneaked back out. Her father had been furious when he'd found out.

Shaking off the nostalgic memories, Izzy stepped to the curb. But Zayn took her by the elbow and kept walking down the sidewalk.

"Aren't we hailing a cab?"

He shook his head. "Nope. What I have in mind is within walking distance."

In no time, they approached what Izzy could only describe as a makeshift Christmas town. Mini wooden chalets lined the walkway, along with stall after stall selling everything from hand-made ornaments to small watercolor paintings.

"Welcome to the Élysées Christmas market," Zayn said, gesturing to the magnificence that surrounded them. "These started out in Germany, but they pop up all over Europe during December."

Izzy found herself at a loss for words. "Oh, my!" was all she could manage.

"What are you in the mood for?" he asked her. "You can pick from all sorts of treats—everything from cheese to biscuits to crêpes."

"It all sounds heavenly."

"Which one?"

She laughed, her senses on overload with complete delight. "All of it. I'd like to try everything."

He winked at her. "That's my girl. Let's start with crêpes."

They spent two hours simply browsing and munching on one treat after another. By the time Zayn led her to the stall of fine chocolates, she could swear she'd never be hungry again. But then she couldn't resist and bit the head off a tiny milk-chocolate soldier.

"That's it," she declared once the soldier's feet were devoured. "Not one more bite."

"Giving up so soon, are you?"

"I'm afraid so. 'Uncle' and all that."

"Wait here," he told her. "There's one more stall I'd like to visit. I'll be right back."'

He strode off without giving her a chance to respond. Just as well, Izzy thought as she waited for him to return, admiring the knit shawls in the next cart over from the chocolate vendor.

She needed a minute to process all she'd just experienced. And to come to terms with the knowledge that she'd just spent the most enjoyable evening of her past five years.

Since Zayn had left.

He'd wanted to get it for her as soon as he'd seen it. Zayn discreetly placed the matchbox-size ornament in his pocket as he rejoined Izzy where she stood waiting for him. He'd give it to her later, when they weren't in a crowded shopping bazaar. Maybe he'd even wait and give it to her when they were back in Napa on Christmas morning, a true holiday gift.

That thought gave him pause. He'd fully intended to fly right back to Manhattan from Paris. Turned out his subconscious had made other plans while he hadn't been paying attention.

Would Izzy even want to spend Christmas with him? He probably shouldn't make assumptions. Was he even ready to ask her? For someone who prided himself on being decisive and action-oriented, he sure seemed to be all over the place when it came to his ex.

They made their way slowly back in the direction of the hotel, walking along the Seine. The city's lights burned bright around them, holiday bulbs adding to the luminescence. In the distance, the Eiffel Tower glowed like a decorative monument to the holiday.

He didn't want the night to end, wanted to somehow capture this moment in time and hold on to it tight. So he paused at the next empty bench, silently led her to it and waited for Izzy to sit. She didn't protest.

Several moments passed in comfortable silence as they both sat watching the river and others strolling along the path. It was like spiraling back in time, the comfort between them, the pure familiarity.

Izzy was the first to break the silence. "This was one of the places we always talked about visiting together."

They'd had any number of dreams back then. Visiting Paris had been one of many.

Izzy chuckled. "How many hours do you suppose we spent talking about all the places we wanted to travel to as soon as we could?"

"Too many to count. It didn't help that my mother would show up occasionally, promising to take me on her next adventure with her. Only to come up with an excuse about why she couldn't."

He hadn't meant to bring up such a somber memory, didn't realize how close to the surface it had been all this time.

Izzy leaned her shoulder against his. No one knew better than her the sheer number of times he'd been disappointed by the mother who'd given birth to him. Izzy had witnessed many of the occasions firsthand. They sat together in silence, Zayn didn't even know for how long, content just to bask in the comfort of having her there beside him. Finally, as the evening grew chillier, he stood and took her hand, pulling her up, too. They resumed walking.

"I don't know why I believed her every time," he found himself admitting. "How did I not learn after being bounced from one home to another each time she promised to pull me out only to not show up?"

He'd lived the life of a nomad, discarded from various relatives and foster guardians, some of them cruelly mean and completely unfit to take care of a child. Finally, his great-aunt Myrna had stepped in once and for all. It had almost been too late. By the time he became a resident of Stackhouse, Zayn had already harbored a level of anger and resentment that no kid should have experienced. Unfortunately, he'd found release in ways that had often landed him in trouble.

"Do you ever hear from your mother?" Izzy asked.

He shrugged. "The occasional birthday card. Or postcard from her latest destination." He tried to recollect her most recent correspondence. It must have come a while ago for he couldn't seem to remember. "I got a wedding invite once. I believe she's married to some sheikh in a small Middle Eastern province. Or maybe she's divorced him since then. I don't really know."

"A sheikh? Huh."

Zayn rubbed his jaw. "Come to think of it, I don't even know my own mother's full name at the moment. If she is indeed remarried, I have no clue what surname she may be carrying."

Then there was his father. A man whose existence Zayn hadn't even thought of until he'd received a strange phone call a few months back. But that was the last thing he wanted to be thinking of right now.

He realized just how much he'd missed Izzy just as a trusted confidante. Someone who listened without judgment, a rarity in his life. Someone who knew him better than anyone else on this earth. And somehow she'd cared for him anyway.

His hand moved toward hers of its own volition. He stopped it just in time, began to clench his fist, only to notice that she'd reached for him, too. Gently, slowly, she wrapped her gloved fingers around his. Holding her hand felt so right and so familiar; the sensation flowed over him like a warm wave.

In the next instant, as if the magic between them had somehow conjured it, large snowflakes began to gently float down from the sky. He couldn't recall a time he'd been in Paris and had it snow. Izzy nudged him and lifted her eyes to the sky, letting the snow fall across her face. A large, fat flake landed on her nose and instantly melted.

Zayn couldn't seem to help himself, he leaned over and kissed the moisture off her skin. She tasted fresh and welcoming and like home.

"Zayn," she whispered his name against his cheek. Part question, part demand. Full of desire.

Heaven help him, he was going to need a cold shower when they made it back to the hotel. Suddenly, he wasn't feeling quite so blasé about the shared suite. As it was, he was ready to pull her into his arms and plunge her mouth, trail kisses along her neck and pull her close against him until he could feel her very breath. Right here, along the path of the river, with crowds of people surrounding them.

The magic and romance of Paris.

He shuddered to think how bad his desire might get when they found themselves alone in the privacy of the suite. Or maybe the shudder had everything to do with how much he wanted her.

Somehow, he managed to pull away and forced his feet to move. Izzy pressed closer against his side.

"I'd forgotten how romantic this city is," she said on a breathless whisper.

He had to acknowledge the implication in her

words. Whether she meant it as such or not, there was the possibility that she was simply overcome with the novelty of being in Paris. Her attraction could be nothing more than the effects of being in this city during the most festive time of the year. Izzy could simply be getting carried away, without a clear thought about what was happening between them.

He should be the responsible one, the one making the right decisions.

And none of that seemed to matter once they made it back to the suite and walked through the door. He'd resolved to bid her good-night then leave the room until she fell asleep. He could try to get some work done in the lobby downstairs. Heck, he could even wander the city aimlessly until all this pent-up emotion within him had a chance to settle.

There was so much to consider—the physical distance between them now that he'd made his home across the country in Manhattan, the sins of the past that he would never be able to tell her, the very real possibility that he'd only end up hurting her again the way he had before. He should know better than to want her.

All those good intentions flew out the window once the door closed behind them. Rather than tell her he was going out for a while, he motioned to the coffee table where housekeeping had left a complimentary bottle of bordeaux.

"Any interest in a nightcap?"

She held his gaze for several moments before answering, heat swimming in her eyes. "I am a little thirsty after all that food and chocolate."

Zayn shrugged off his coat and made his way farther into the room. Izzy curled up on the couch and tucked her feet underneath her. She hadn't taken off his scarf. Her hair draped in glorious waves over where she'd wrapped it around her neck. He wanted to reach for her, remove the scarf, then continue disrobing her until she was bare and trembling in his arms. His breath caught at the image and he forced himself to look away and grab the wine.

But when he looked over at her again after uncorking the bottle, her lids were closed and she was breathing evenly. She'd fallen asleep.

Zayn didn't know whether he was more disappointed or relieved.

Izzy felt herself being lifted off the couch and carried by a set of solid, strong arms.

"I'm not asleep," she protested. "Just closed my eyes for a bit."

"If you weren't asleep, you were fast approaching getting there," Zayn's deep, rich voice answered.

"Besides, I thought we'd established that I'd be sleeping on the couch." Though now that she said it, she found the notion held absolutely no appeal. Heaven help her, she didn't want to be across the room from Zayn on a hard, antique sofa. She wanted to be where he was. In his bed.

"We established no such thing."

They'd reached the bed. Izzy met his eyes and her breath caught in her throat at the heat that swam in them. Desire flooded their depths. Desire for her. He wanted her. It was as clear as the bright lights shining outside their balcony door. Her own need burned just as strong.

Her gaze fell to his lips. So close, his mouth was a shallow breath away from hers. "Zayn?" She could only say his name.

His hold on her tightened. She could feel every beat of his heart against the skin of her cheek. Her own heartbeat echoed in her ears. She slid down until her feet touched the floor, her body full against the length of him. Wrapping her arms around his neck, she stood on tiptoe to even their height difference. He swallowed. "Iz, I'm not so—"

She pressed her fingers to his lips to stop him from going further. She didn't need to hear any words right now. She only needed one thing.

"Sweetheart…" he began. "I'm trying really hard here to stay true to what I said earlier about being a gentleman. You're not exactly making it easy."

"I think I'd be sorely disappointed if you were finding it easy."

Then she couldn't think at all as he pulled her tighter against his chest. Her body was crushed against his and it felt exquisite. His hands moved down her back, lower, until he cupped her bottom, pulling her up until she could clearly feel the strength of his desire.

It made her heady to know how much he wanted her, how powerful his need for her was. His hands roamed over her body, burning a trail of fire wherever he touched her.

It had been so long. And she'd missed him so much.

Consequences be damned. She would worry about those later.

CHAPTER TEN

HE'D DREAMED ABOUT THIS, thought about it more often than he should have over the years. Holding her again, tasting her, feeling her luscious curves against him. In his imaginings, he managed to go slow, take his time, start with a small and gentle kiss then trail further kisses along her chin and down her neck. Fully in control of himself. How naïve of him.

Reality turned out to be very different. He'd thought he'd have more restraint if he ever got to touch her again. But he was barely hanging on to any semblance of restraint at the moment.

This is how things had always been between them. Passion and fire and pure want combusting in a powerful force until neither one of them could think straight. In fact, he didn't think he could form another coherent thought for as long as he lived.

He none-too-gently nudged her onto the bed beneath him, limbs intertwined. Her breath gasped against his chin and then her hands began torturing him. She ran her fingers up his chest, palmed over his shoulders then moved back down, lower and lower until he thought he'd stop breathing. All the while, he couldn't get enough of her mouth on his. When she cried out his name again against his mouth, he thought he might die from need.

It took seconds for their clothes to end up in a haphazard pile on the floor. One of her buttons tore free and rolled off the bed. How could he have ever thought he could resist her when he saw her again?

He wanted to slow things down, but it was all out of his control. He was mere clay in her skilled, capable hands. Izzy was solidly at the helm. And he was going to let her lead.

Tonight, he would follow anywhere she took him.

She woke up exhausted and mildly achy the next morning, albeit in an entirely pleasurable way. It also appeared she'd woken up alone.

Bolting upright on the bed, Izzy glanced around for any sign of Zayn. She'd had dreams of rousing out of sleep embraced in his arms, proceeding to take up where they'd last left things.

Her cell phone lit up on the bedside table with

a text message. Ran out to get you pastries and fresh rolls for breakfast. Don't go anywhere. He'd added several emojis at the end, some of them rather naughty. Definitely not the standard set that came already loaded on the smartphone. A couple at the end brought a blush to her cheeks and reminded her of the previous night. Those thoughts only led to further blushing.

Zayn certainly seemed to bring out a side of her that she didn't usually let loose. She felt comfortable with him. He'd been her first real boyfriend and anyone she'd dated in between hadn't stood a chance against what she felt for him.

Izzy swore and plopped over onto her back. Now that morning light was shedding some clarity on things, nagging thoughts bordered the edges of her mind. Did she really know what she was getting herself into here?

She'd been crushed when he'd left. Her heart had been irreparably damaged. It had taken her months to begin to feel like herself again. And years to so much as start dating other men. None of those relationships had taken root.

Now she was lying in a warm bed in Paris and Zayn was sending her sexy text messages. They'd spent all night in each other's arms. As if the last five years had never happened.

But they had.

And she still didn't have any answers.

Or perhaps she did. Maybe what he'd told her the day he'd left really was all there was to it. Maybe his silence all the time since then was answer enough.

That he'd left because Napa was too small for him, the town held too many bad memories.

Maybe he had left her to become the global professional success that he was today. And maybe their relationship had always meant more to her than it had ever meant to him.

So what did all those possibilities mean for where they stood today? More specifically, what did it mean for her that she'd fallen into Zayn's bed within a week of seeing him again? The charms and enchantments of Paris during Christmas were no excuse.

The truth was she didn't have any kind of excuse. She had to accept that. Had to accept the reality that she hadn't gotten over the man despite all the time that had passed. She probably never would get over him.

Suddenly her appetite for pastries or anything else had completely disintegrated. Despite Zayn's directive to stay put, she got up to shower and get dressed. It was time to be brutally honest with herself. When it came to this particular man, she would always lead with her heart. Even if it ultimately meant getting it torn to shreds. It was high time for her to decide, once and for all, what she planned to do about it.

Could she be the type of woman who could take whatever was offered by the man she loved? Because she did love him; there was no denying that anymore. Another thing she had to come to terms with: Zayn's reappearance in her life was temporary. After this trip, she may never see him again.

You could be a big girl and take what life... and Zayn...have to offer. Try to enjoy what you can have rather than wallow about all that you can't.

She'd never been the type of woman who could do relationships without emotional involvement. But if there was anyone on earth who might tempt her to do just that, he was the one whose toiletries lay strewed all over the bathroom she'd just entered.

When she emerged half an hour later, the suite was still empty. Except there was a cardboard box tied with pastry string sitting on the coffee table. No sign of Zayn.

She went to check her phone and, sure enough, there was a message.

Sorry, got called away on an emergency conference call that I decided to take in the hotel's

VIP business lounge. Let's meet for lunch at the Eiffel Tower. Can't wait to see you!

No playful emojis this time. See, maybe this was some kind of sign. The morning after they'd fallen back into bed together and they couldn't even connect in person. Quickly typing an affirmative reply, she pushed away her disappointment at the delay.

The phone pinged again before she could even set it down.

Still stuck on this call but wanted to send you this. I'm so proud of you!

The text had an attachment from the expo brochure. They'd highlighted her cabernet in a write-up about the awards ceremony.

A completely unwelcome pang of longing settled in her chest. He was proud of her. His accolade shouldn't have meant as much as it did. She knew her wine's nomination was a fluky thing akin to winning the state lottery. Not that she wasn't proud of her work, she absolutely took great pride in it. But her pride and dedication weren't dependent on some industry award she'd randomly been selected for because a tourist to her tasting room happened to work for a beverage magazine. Stackhouse wasn't the type of winery that normally warranted that kind of attention. And that was fine with her. She liked that it was relatively a non-player, with visits by appointment only and cases that sold out every year because their entire operation was small. All the qualities that had driven Zayn to want to buy her out in the first place.

She stared at his words again on her screen. Did he mean he was proud of her as a business partner? Or as the woman he… She didn't even know how to categorize what she might mean to him. For all she knew, her feelings were completely one-sided and there was nothing more than physical attraction where Zayn was concerned. She might have thought to ask him before sleeping with the man last night.

Well, she was done wallowing in self-pity and drowning in questions. She was here for an expo and there were panels to attend and wines to taste. She was a professional vintner on a business trip and she needed to act like it.

She picked up the hotel phone to order a pot of hot French roast to go alongside the pastries. Then, putting her hair up in a tight bun and pulling out a pencil skirt business suit, she dressed and began preparing for her day.

Heaven help her, she had no idea what she intended to say to Zayn when she saw him in a few hours. Or how she would resist running into his arms the moment she laid eyes on him.

He shouldn't have even bothered with that conference call. The emergency turned out to be an overblown crisis spurned by a panicked employee. And it wasn't as if he'd been able to pay any kind of close attention to what was being said. That's why he'd opted to take the call in the lounge in the first place; he'd known being in the same room with Izzy would have proved much too distracting.

What a shameful waste of time. He would have much preferred to spend the morning the same way he'd spent most of the night, with Izzy snuggled up close to him in bed. Not that that's what they'd been doing for most of the time.

He could hardly wait to see her again.

Though he was starting to rethink this plan of his to meet her for lunch at the Eiffel Tower. What had he been thinking this morning when he'd sent her that text? He should have told her to take off every article of clothing and wait for him in the hotel room wearing nothing but the scarf he'd let her borrow yesterday. The scarf and nothing else. Perhaps he could ask her for a rain check on that score.

Hastening his pace, he glanced at his watch.

He was running a few minutes late, hated the thought that he might be keeping her waiting. But when he reached the square, he realized he'd been harried for no reason.

Izzy was nowhere to be found. Had she forgotten? She was one of the most prompt and time-conscious people he knew. Or at least, she had been. What did he really know anymore about her? People changed a lot in five years. Look at all the changes he'd made for himself. One could argue he was a completely different person.

It was foolish of him to think that Izzy was the same loyal, unaffected person she'd been when he'd walked away. For all he knew, she'd turned into the kind of woman who forgot lunch dates she'd made the next day with men she'd spent the night with.

The thoughts scurrying through his brain had him gripping his phone so tight, he actually felt the screen bend.

Get hold of yourself. She was probably just running late, the same as he had been. It was only about fifteen minutes past their agreed-upon time. She'd probably been distracted at a panel back at the conference center or on the way here doing some impromptu window-shopping. Paris boutiques could have that sort of effect on women; he'd witnessed it firsthand on some of his previous visits with others.

He fished his phone out of his pocket to check for last-minute messages. Nothing. Not from her, anyway.

Looking around the square proved futile. She wasn't there. The familiar quickening of his breath sent a surge of annoyance through him. This was no time to have one of those damn episodes—or whatever they were. They'd been plaguing him for the better part of two years now and they'd grown more frequent and more bothersome.

He refused to be distracted by one right now. This was so not the time.

Loosening his grip on the phone, he started to pull up Izzy's contact info. There was also the possibility to consider that she may have gotten lost. Paris wasn't exactly a familiar city for her. He should have made sure to tell her to take the car and driver he had on standby with the hotel. Some parts of the city were definitely seedier than others. He clicked on her number and waited, his breath hitching in near panic. He'd never forgive himself if harm had happened to come to her.

The call immediately went to her voice mail. Zayn bit out a curse. He should never have left her alone in an unfamiliar city. What had he been thinking?

A familiar voice sounded from behind him before he could dial her again.

"Zayn, here I am." She ran up to him, rosy-cheeked and near huffing for air. "Were you waiting long? I'm so sorry. I was doing some shopping." She held up a parcel. "The French salesladies definitely make it a leisurely affair. They serve cookies and everything as they wait on you. Took forever to try on dresses and find one I liked."

She stopped to study his face. "What's the matter? You look a little pale."

The relief he felt surging through his system kept him from answering right away. Now that the scare was over, he felt rather foolish for jumping to so many erroneous and perilous scenarios in his mind.

"I thought you might have gotten lost. Wasn't sure whether I should start looking for you."

"I'm so sorry," she repeated. "I didn't realize the shopping would take so long. And then I underestimated the time it would take to walk over here. I'm not terribly familiar with the city."

Zayn closed his eyes and took a calming breath. "It's okay, Iz. I just started to worry. Then when you didn't answer your phone…"

Her face brightened once more and she

hooked her arm through his elbow. "You were worried about me, huh?"

He forced a smile through the tense muscles around his mouth. "Maybe a little." He took the bag from her hand and led her toward the opposite side of the square and the small bistro he had in mind for lunch. He could use a sit-down with a nice cold glass of chardonnay.

Izzy paused before the second step. "Wait. Do you mind if we do a quick climb of the tower first? I haven't been here since they debuted the glass floor and I've been so looking forward to seeing it. I'm not terribly hungry just yet."

He took a moment too long to answer.

"Unless you're hungry right now," she hastily added at his hesitation.

Zayn forced some air into his lungs and wrangled some calm. "Of course, we can visit the tower. Anything you wish."

What he really needed was to sit and gather himself in a quiet, peaceful spot like the bistro. But the smile Izzy flashed him made it hard to deny her.

"We're lucky it's not terribly crowded today," Zayn said next to her. He'd taken her hand and still carried her package.

Given the rather cloudy day, there weren't as many tourists visiting the tower. Izzy let Zayn lead her into the small crowd of other visitors. The line moved slowly but pretty steadily. She stole a sideways glance at his profile. There was something off about him; he didn't seem his usual, assured self. He appeared distracted, anxious.

Must have been something to do with his emergency call earlier. She felt guilty for having alarmed him at all by being late. The truth was she'd had no intention of doing any shopping. She'd packed everything she'd needed, including a sensible, casual black wrap dress to wear to the awards ceremony. But that text had made her rethink her options. Zayn had said he was proud of her. He'd be with her at the dinner event as they announced the winner. Suddenly, she'd cared about dressing up for it, wanted something more than the boring outfit she'd purchased off the discount rack at a department store back home. She was in the fashion mecca of the world, surely it was worth a look.

But she'd ended up alarming Zayn. Though why he'd been worked up over her being a few minutes late was something of a mystery. It took about ten minutes for them to reach the base of the tower. They bustled into the elevator and got off on the first level.

"The last time I was in France, I didn't get a

chance to do much sightseeing," she explained. "Thank you for indulging me."

"You're welcome, Iz."

Izzy squealed in delight as she walked out onto the deck. This first level was the one with the see-through glass floor panels. They were about two hundred feet off the ground and the people below looked like little ants. Izzy felt like she was walking on air.

The feeling of standing on the glass was a little disconcerting. She gingerly stepped closer to the edge, staring at the view below her feet. Though confident it was safe, her lizard brain cried out a warning that she shouldn't be this high off the ground and be able to see the world below.

Something fell to the floor behind her. She looked over to see that Zayn had dropped her package. He was as white as a bedsheet. Rushing to his side, she grabbed him by the arm.

"Zayn? What's the matter?"

He swallowed hard. "Nothing. I'm fine."

He clearly wasn't. A smile spread over his lips that appeared forced and fake.

"You've gone very pale," she told him, concern flooding her chest.

"Have I?" He appeared to be studying her as he spoke, hyperfocused on her face. As if he were afraid to let his eyes travel anywhere else. "The glass floor just threw me off, that's all. Feeling a bit dizzy."

She could only nod. He certainly wasn't the only person here who appeared to be experiencing a touch of vertigo. But a nagging voice was telling her there was more going on. Zayn's pallor had started turning a concerning hue of green. She thought she might have heard him muttering numbers under his breath.

"Perhaps you're coming down with something?" she ventured.

He gave a small nod. "Hope not. I have a rather busy couple of weeks ahead of me. Don't have time to catch a cold." He tried to uphold the fake smile but the effect came off as more of a grimace.

"Have you had breakfast?"

He shook his head. "No, I haven't eaten yet today. I'm sure that isn't helping."

Her guilt multiplied by several factors. First, she'd had him worried by making him wait, then she'd ask to delay lunch even longer. This after the man had hand-delivered breakfast to her and then made reservations for lunch.

"Oh, Zayn. I wish you'd told me you were starving. We could have gone straight to eat." Leaning down, she picked up the package he'd dropped. Zayn stared at it as if seeing it for the first time. He didn't even seem to be aware that it had slipped out of his hand.

Alarm bells began ringing in Izzy's head. She nudged him gently ahead of her toward the elevator.

Looked like their Eiffel Tower visit was over. "Let's get you back on solid ground."

He immediately began to protest. "No, I don't want to be the reason you don't get to tour the Eiffel Tower, Izzy. I'm fine to go on to the top."

Was he serious? He appeared to be in no condition to continue standing, let alone do any more sightseeing with her. "We have a couple more days in Paris," she reassured him. "I'll make you come back with me when you're up for it. After you've eaten something."

Izzy swallowed past the concern rising in her chest. Zayn was one of the strongest, most virile, men she knew. It was unsettling to see him the way he was right now. But her main focus at the moment was to get him out of the bustle of tower visitors and back to the first floor. It seemed to take forever, but finally they made it outside and onto a bench. She quickly stopped to purchase a bottle of water from a vendor along the way.

By the time they were seated, she was relieved to see some of the color return to his face.

He appeared less ashen, less shaky. She handed him the water.

Izzy blew out the breath she'd been holding as he took a sip. "Are you feeling better?"

He gave her a wry smile. "Nothing hurts now but my pride. Who knew I suffered from vertigo?"

"Is that what that was?"

"Had to be. I'm otherwise fit as a fiddle. Let's go eat, shall we?" With that, he stood and reached his hand out for her to take. He certainly seemed to be feeling better. And the recovery had happened so quickly that she supposed it must have been a temporary touch of vertigo. It made sense based on the fact that they had been literally standing on glass several floors above the ground. Not everyone was cut out for such a visual. Right now, he appeared recovered and energetic.

She took Zayn's hand and stood.

CHAPTER ELEVEN

How mortifying.

So much for being the dashing and suave gentleman who had whisked his ex-girlfriend to Paris. Zayn waited for Izzy to sit at the corner table the greeter had led them to before taking a chair himself. He hadn't had an episode that bad in as long as he could remember. Just his luck it had to happen in front of Izzy. She was still watching him with guarded scrutiny.

"You look adorable when you're worried. Particularly, when it's me you're worried about." It was a rather lame attempt to lighten the moment, which didn't seem to work judging by the concern still clouding her eyes.

"I can't help it, Zayn. Are you sure you're all right? Is this because of the mishap with Frosty?"

That question was so preposterous he almost had to laugh. "No. Definitely not."

He had to give her something, he supposed.

"Nothing to fret about, Iz. It's just something that happens occasionally."

Her eyes grew wide. Rather than placating her, his words appeared to have further edged her concern. "You mean this has happened before?"

He nodded. "Started a couple of years ago."

"Why haven't you had it checked?" she wanted to know.

She should give him more credit than that. "I have. In fact, I went in for a complete workup before I flew to Napa."

"And?"

"Nothing out of the ordinary. Was told to try to relax more. Cut down on stress and take more vacations." He didn't have to tell her he could pinpoint exactly when the episodes had started. She didn't have to know that the very first one had been triggered by a phone call he'd received out of the blue one fateful day. A call he would have never imagined getting. From a man he'd never expected to hear from. His absentee father who'd apparently suddenly had a change of heart.

No, he didn't want to get into all of that with Izzy. He didn't even want to think about it. Or the myriad reasons he'd clicked off the call before the old man could finish saying whatever it was he'd had to say. Nor why Zayn had ignored his repeated attempts to reach him again afterward. He'd eventually blocked the number. Only to have a different one call his phone a few weeks after he'd done so.

She reached across the table. "Zayn, I think you've been having anxiety attacks."

The waiter chose that moment to hand them their menus and fill their glasses with ice water. Izzy didn't let go of his hand.

He waved off the suggestion. His own doctor had tried to tell him something similar. What difference did it make what the clinical term was? He'd been burning the proverbial candle at both ends for years now and those blasted phone calls had simply tipped things over the edge.

In any case, he didn't have time to deal with it. "Nah, I just need to slow down."

She didn't seem convinced. "Maybe when we get back you can go see Ethan—"

He held a hand up to stop her before she could go any further. No way in the world he was going to discuss his shortcomings with anyone from his past. And especially not Izzy.

"No," he stated simply.

"Why not?" she pressed. "It's not something to be ashamed of."

Zayn pulled his hand out of her grip. "Honestly, Izzy. You don't have to concern yourself with this." His tone sounded sharper than he'd intended. But he really was tired of discussing it. If the episodes didn't stop on their own eventually, he would deal with it when he had time.

She pursed her lips before speaking. "In other words, it's none of my business."

"That's not what I said, Iz. Let's just enjoy our lunch for now." He opened up the cloth-covered menu. "This place is known for its duck à l'orange. I'll get a bottle of champagne to go with it."

She didn't make a move to look at her own menu. She just wasn't going to let this go.

Zayn sighed and rubbed his forehead. "Would it make you feel better if I promise to take a vacation when I get back to the States?"

"Maybe." She shrugged an elegant shoulder. "It would be a start, I suppose," she added begrudgingly.

"Then I promise to do just that."

"I'm not so sure you know how to relax, Zayn. How do I know you wouldn't just work through your vacation?"

She knew him too well, probably better than anyone else on the planet. He chuckled. "Would you like me to sign a contract?"

She leaned over the table. "This is not a laughing matter, Zayn. I wish you would take it more seriously."

He wanted to put her mind at ease. He really

did. He could only think of one way that might appease her for the short term.

"How about I prove to you that I can take it easy and take time off?"

She lifted her chin, silently scrutinizing his words. "How do you propose to do that exactly?"

"After your ceremony tonight, I say we beg off the rest of this expo. We have two more days in Paris. Let's turn it into a vacation of sorts. Then I can show you firsthand that I'm taking time off."

He certainly seemed to have her attention. "Go on. I'm listening."

Now that he was saying the words out loud, he was growing keener and keener on the idea. "For the next two days we become full-blown, bona fide tourists. Nothing but sightseeing, fun and frivolity."

Finally, a small smile seemed to creep onto her face. "How do I know this isn't simply a shameless attempt to get me to spend more time in hotel rooms with you?"

"Not shameless at all," he teased. "I fully admit to being guilty on that count—that thought had indeed crossed my mind."

She steepled her fingers on the table, considering. Zayn actually caught himself moving to the edge of his seat awaiting her answer. Finally she blew out a puff of air. "All right. Let's do it. Why not?"

Clasping a hand to his chest in mock despair, he grinned at her. "Not the most enthusiastic acceptance, but I'll have to take it."

He was ridiculously pleased at the unexpected turn of events. For the next two days, he'd have Izzy all to himself in one of the loveliest countries on the planet.

A man couldn't ask for much more.

For an awards ceremony she didn't particularly feel invested in, Izzy found herself spending quite some time standing in front of a mirror to get ready.

What exactly had she agreed to at lunch?

She'd been so concerned about Zayn, she probably would have agreed to anything. If he really did need a break that badly—and, judging by the severity of the panic attack she'd witnessed, he clearly did—then she would see to it that he took a couple of days off. Besides, a girl could do worse than to spend two days playing tourist throughout France.

First, they had to get through this ceremony tonight. She didn't get many opportunities to dress up in a formal evening gown. This was a bit of a novelty. The dress she'd bought on impulse this afternoon hung on the back of the bathroom door as she toyed with her hair.

What in the world would she say if she happened to win? From what she'd been told, the winner was expected to go up on stage to accept the trophy. Like the Oscars. Or Grammys.

There was a possibility, albeit she believed it to be slim, that it very well could be her.

Ha! Fat chance. There were at least a dozen nominees altogether. The chances of her coming out on top were slim to none. Some of the wines she was up against were masterpieces from some of the most renowned vineyards in Europe.

Okay. So maybe she was more nervous about this ceremony than she was allowing herself to believe. When she'd first been notified of the honor, she'd been too busy with all her new responsibilities and reeling in the middle of grieving the loss of Myrna. Now that the time was here and reality stared her in the face, she had to acknowledge that this was actually a pretty big deal.

I'm so proud of you.

Win or not, Zayn was impressed with her. The thought shouldn't thrill her as much as it did. But he had her worried. Whatever was going on with him, she planned to do her best to get to the bottom of it. It wouldn't be easy; she could guess he wasn't going to let her in. All the more reason to believe he wasn't after anything serious as far as the two of them were concerned.

Yet she wanted to make sure he was okay. And she'd have two days to observe and take notice if he had another episode. She'd work on convincing him to seek better treatment, as well.

But tonight...tonight was another matter. Tonight she was going to dress up and attend a fancy ceremony on the arm of a handsome and charming entrepreneur while she sipped fancy champagne and enjoyed herself.

Almost like some kind of date.

Stop it. She was being silly. That's what happened when you hadn't gone out in ages with anyone resembling a romantic interest. Still, would it be so wrong of her to play pretend? She glanced at the dress once more. Strapless, with tiny hints of glitter intertwined in the silly fabric. The color was a rich midnight-blue that shouldn't have worked with her coloring but somehow did. Just as the saleslady had assured her it would. Paula had loaned her a pair of stilettos as she'd never owned a pair in her life. Black-leather straps with two-inch heels she'd be lucky not to trip in.

Between the dress and the shoes, the outfit was so unlike anything she would normally wear.

Like the saying went, when in France and all that.

* * *

Zayn adjusted his collar and clipped on the gold cuff links he'd brought along specifically for this event. Normally, black tie affairs bored him to tears, but he found himself looking forward to this one. That feeling had everything to do with the company he'd be keeping.

A twinge of guilt made him wince when he thought about all that had happened earlier that afternoon at the tower. He'd given Izzy quite a scare. He owed it to her to try to make that right. Part of the reason he'd wanted to whisk her away for some fun and sightseeing while they were here.

The shower had gone off a while ago but Izzy was still in the bathroom. He'd been tempted to knock on the door, in the hope of catching her as she toweled off. He could help her get dry, running the Turkish towel over every inch of her before lifting her and carrying her to the bed.

He shut his eyes to force out the images. They had an awards ceremony to get to. He couldn't make her late when she was one of the nominees, as appealing as that idea was.

He found himself surprised at how long it was taking her to get ready. It wasn't like Izzy to spend too much time prepping and fussing. Though, admittedly, this was a rather special occasion.

When they'd been kids, Izzy had always leaned toward an understated style of dress, bordering on tomboy. She'd still always managed to look feminine and alluring. Torn jeans or black yoga pants with baggy shirts or tanks. It would be interesting to see her in anything formal.

Only "interesting" didn't even begin to cover it when she revealed herself. He wasn't prepared for what he saw when she finally stepped out. His mouth went dry at the sight of her.

The dress existed to be on her skin, as if it had been created for her and her alone. Deep, dark blue, the color reminded him of a starless night in the height of summer. There was a slit that went up her leg several inches above her knee. Heaven help him, his hand itched to run his palm up the gap and then go higher. Her hair—she'd done something complicated with it. It was piled high atop her head with delicate tendrils loose around her face. And heels. He was pretty sure he'd never seen her in heels before.

She looked sexy as hell.

"I'm sorry if that took a while. I'm not used to getting dolled up. Don't really know what I'm doing."

She was clearly a fast learner. He could only nod in response.

She rubbed a hand down her middle and did

a little twirl. "Well, what do you think? Will this work?"

He remained silent so long, she started to fidget. But he couldn't seem to get his mouth to work. Finally, he found his tongue and managed to answer.

"Oh, yeah. It works, all right. It works very, very well."

She hardly recognized herself. Who was this person so effortlessly mingling among the stars of the international wine community? It was almost as if she actually belonged among them.

Much of the credit for her confidence went to Zayn. He kept feeding her positive reinforcement as they moved along the crowd to their assigned table. She introduced herself to a couple of the magazine editors, one fellow vintner from Spain and an American distributor. She even threw in some high school French while speaking and managed to stay balanced on the stiletto heels that felt totally alien on her feet.

The reception was being held in the banquet room of a deluxe restaurant in the heart of Paris. Christmas decorations adorned the walls and mini decorated trees served as centerpieces on the tables. Two wine fountains had been set up in opposite corners of the room, one for white and one for red. Hovering servers, dressed in tuxedo vests and pressed slacks, carried trays of hors d'oeuvres among the crowd.

"This is the fanciest dinner I've ever attended," she admitted to Zayn as they took their seats.

He sat next to her after helping her into her own chair. "Just think, you're one of the guests of honor."

A nervous flutter tickled the center of her stomach. She'd have to apologize to her brother when she returned home. If it wasn't for Hector, she would have completely missed all this. She owed him a debt of gratitude for his persistence. As she did with Zayn. He'd played no small role in getting her here.

She stole a glance at him now for what must have been the hundredth time since they'd left the hotel. The man looked like he could be featured in a yacht ad or in a Billionaire Bachelor calendar spread. The formal tuxedo he wore must have been custom made for him. It fit him perfectly, accentuating his toned physique and wide shoulders. While such extravagant surroundings were so new to her, he was clearly in his element. This was a whole different world for her, but there was no question a man like Zayn belonged with a crowd such as the one they were in. If anything, he commanded the room with his presence.

Now, with the barest nod of his head, he summoned one of the servers who brought over a tray of bubbly champagne. Taking two flutes off the tray, he handed her one then lifted his.

"A toast, to you and the cabernet you've created."

"Don't toast me yet," she protested. "I haven't actually won anything."

"You're already a winner as far as I'm concerned."

Their tablemates arrived at that very moment. An older couple impeccably dressed.

"Oh, how romantic," the silver-haired woman said in perfect English as her husband pulled out her chair. "If you don't mind my saying," she continued, taking her seat, "you two are quite a charming couple."

Izzy didn't get a chance to form a response before Zayn immediately corrected the statement.

"Thank you, ma'am. But we happen to be business partners, nothing more." He went on to tell her where they were from and bragged about her nomination.

Izzy couldn't help the bristle that skimmed over her skin. He was so quick to set the record straight, even to a couple of strangers they would most likely never see again after tonight.

"I beg your pardon for the misunderstanding, then," the woman said with a smile. "But I stand by what I said," she added rather cheekily.

Izzy took another sip of champagne. Silly, really, to feel out of sorts at the exchange. Zayn hadn't said anything incorrect. It was nothing but foolishness on her part that she let it bother her in the least.

The lights dimmed ever so slightly as the ceremony began.

There were so many different categories, Izzy found it hard to pay attention. Everything from best barrel maker to adherence to organic practices was considered for an award.

Finally, when time came to announce the cabernet winner, she thought her heart might pound right out of her chest.

But it wasn't her name that was called. Someone else, a rather plump man from Argentina was the lucky recipient. Izzy tried to clamp down on her disappointment. She hadn't really expected to win; the competition was too stiff. Still, it would have been nice to bring the miniature glass bottle trophy home. This was exactly why she hadn't dared to hope. Except that it turned out she actually had.

She felt Zayn give her knee a squeeze under the table. His support was something of a buffer, one she did appreciate.

He leaned over to whisper in her ear. "You'll get 'em next time, Iz."

The chance of being nominated again was not something she was going to hang her hat on. One day she'd be able to appreciate the honor of simply being nominated. Right now, she just wanted to wallow in disappointment for a while.

Two hours later, when the ceremony was over and the lights returned to full brightness, she was more than ready to leave.

What had started out as an exciting night full of potential had turned into nothing more than a major letdown.

She couldn't even be sure if she was referring to the loss or to Zayn's abject dismissal of them being described as any kind of couple.

Though truth be told, one definitely stung more than the other.

CHAPTER TWELVE

SHE PRETENDED TO SLEEP in the car on the ride back to the hotel. She was in no mood to talk. The day felt like it had gone on hours too long. Had it really been just this afternoon when they'd attempted to tour the Eiffel Tower?

If Zayn knew she was faking, to his credit, he wasn't calling her on it. Probably thought she was crushed by her defeat. Little did he know, that was only part of her disappointment this evening.

She fully intended to continue the charade until she heard him say something in French to the driver. *"Arrêtez, si'l vous plait."* He was asking him to stop the car.

Izzy opened her eyes.

"Sleeping Beauty awakens," Zayn said with a soft smile.

Hadn't she required a kiss first? She probably shouldn't bring that up. "Just resting my eyes. It's been a long day. Why are we stopping?"

He pointed outside her window. "We happen to be driving by the Champs-Élysées."

"Why would we want to stop here?" The question was answered as soon as she turned to look behind her. The sight was breathtaking—an extravaganza of lights. There had to be millions of tiny bulbs set up like works of art. She gasped as the color theme changed from blue to red then a brilliant green.

Zayn shifted in the seat to move closer to her. "I figured we might start our minivacation here and now. If you're up for it."

Despite her aching feet—how did women wear such pointy heels on the regular?—and despite her general tiredness, she suddenly felt a surge of energy. She had to see it up close.

Zayn led her out of the car and over to the display. Despite the late hour and the December chill, there was a good number of people admiring it along with her. It was easy to see the draw. The effect was like watching fireworks suspended right there on the ground.

"This is a masterpiece," she said on a breathless sigh.

"I thought you'd like to see it. Every year they seem to outdo themselves from the year before."

It was hard to decide where to look. Orbs and spirals and geometric shapes presented like a visual banquet. Though it would never capture the true magic on display, Izzy fished out the smartphone from her clutch purse and snapped a picture. "No wonder you weren't impressed with my light-up snowman."

He chuckled. "In my defense, the snowman did try to kill me."

"I'm terribly sorry about that," she apologized, though it sounded rather insincere considering the words were muffled by a giggle she couldn't help. "He's been reformed."

"Then I can relate." His words held a wealth of meaning, she knew. Zayn's history of getting into trouble ran the gamut with everything from disorderly conduct to disturbing the peace. As well as a few bar fights in between. He really had turned himself around as an adult.

"You're a true American success story, Zayn. Resident bad boy turned billionaire entrepreneur. The stuff of legends."

He scoffed at that. "I made some smart business decisions after working my behind off for a few years."

She wondered if the sheer tenacity required for such a transformation had had anything to do with the bouts of anxiety that were now plaguing him. But he'd made it clear at lunch he didn't want to talk about his episode. And she didn't want to ruin this moment by pressing.

Besides, as he'd made very clear to their

tablemates earlier tonight, there was nothing between them but a business partnership. So it was clearly none of her business.

Never mind that they'd spent their first night in Paris in the deepest throes of passion, unable to get enough of each other.

"Were you terribly disappointed? About losing tonight?" he asked.

Zayn had a tendency to change the subject when it veered toward him for too long.

"More so than I would have thought," she admitted. "But I'm slowly getting over it."

"There'll be other awards, Izzy. This nomination put you on the map. You're an internationally recognized name now."

"Are you saying that as my business partner?" she couldn't resist asking.

The lights before them changed color again, this time transforming into a brilliant shade of silver. Izzy felt as if she were standing in the middle of a constellation of stars.

"Did that bother you? My saying that?"

She simply raised a shoulder.

"We were at an event thrown by a magazine. There were at least three photographers there. I didn't want the attention and gossip that any innuendo of a relationship between the two owners of Stackhouse Winery might lead to."

Well, when he put it that way, she supposed

he had a point. A spark of hope began to heat in her chest. So he'd had a good reason for shooting down the older lady's assessment of them as a romantic couple.

His next words were like a bucket of cold water thrown over the flame. "But you bring up a good point. The fact is we are still business partners."

And apparently that was the part of their relationship Zayn wanted to focus on. Despite the fact that they'd slept together last night. "And we have very different ideas about how to run things."

"You're not telling me anything I don't know."

He crossed his arms in front of his chest. "You know as well as I do that, at some point, we are going to have to figure out how to reconcile those differences, Izzy. For the sake of the winery and it's bottom line."

Of course, she knew that. What she had no idea about was how she was going to reconcile her heart when Zayn walked away from her again once the business affairs were finally put in order.

They were both too tired and spent to do much more than take turns brushing their teeth then collapsing onto the bed when they returned to the suite close to midnight.

As much as he wanted her, and as much a temptation as she was curled up on the mattress next to him, Zayn was more than content just to be able to watch her sleep.

In hindsight, he knew he should have never touched her. He should have kept a tight rein on his control the night before, despite the strong desire that had clearly never waned over the past five years.

He'd just missed her so much.

Still, he should have slept on the damn couch. Or, better yet, in the marble bathtub in the bathroom, with the door securely locked to keep from succumbing to temptation.

There was too much baggage between them, too much unresolved. They still hadn't figured out how they were going to move forward as co-owners of Stackhouse. He had no doubt now that Izzy would never agree to sell her share. In hindsight, it had been foolish of him to ever think otherwise. And this past week, after seeing her in action, he had to admit Stackhouse needed her at the helm. But he still disagreed with the general business model the winery operated under. That meant they would have to somehow find a way to compromise. Not exactly a history of success between them in that regard.

Then there was the matter of her father. If Zayn had ever been tempted to tell her the truth about why he'd left Napa and the part Ernesto had played in his decision, there was absolutely no way he could give in to that temptation now. There was already a rift between father and daughter that was clearly hurting Izzy. He would never forgive himself for having any part in widening that rift any further.

It was all so messy. Sleeping together had only complicated things further. He had no idea what to do about it now.

Water under the bridge. What's done was done. And a million other clichés that could also apply.

He had two more days with Izzy before reality came back to retrieve him like the ghost of Christmas Present from that play featured in every metropolitan city theater during the holiday season. He vowed to make the most of these two days. After that, he needed to leave her alone to live the rewarding, peaceful life she deserved.

A life that included friends, family and career fulfillment. One that unfortunately couldn't include him.

Because, unlike the character in that play, he'd never fully been able to get away from his own ghosts of the past.

The next morning, he had the driver drop them off at the gold-colored gates of Château de Versailles. He'd promised her two full days of tourist excursions and Zayn figured the palace was the perfect place to start. Though seeing Versailles in the middle of winter wasn't ideal—one couldn't truly appreciate the gardens or the statues outside—the château itself was as grand as it ever was during the year.

He would have to bring Izzy back during the warmer months.

Whoa. Where had that thought come from? He had no business making any future plans that involved her. Hadn't he settled all that last night?

He led her through the entrance and Izzy gasped when they moved into the front garden. "Oh, my."

"It's lovely, isn't it? In summer, it's even more of a sight to behold." The fountain wasn't running and tarp covered many of the statues and bushes.

"It's spectacular." Her fingers covered her mouth as she looked on in awe. He loved seeing that look of wonder in her eyes. She'd always been very visual. He'd always wondered why she'd never taken up art.

Perhaps the creativity that went into producing a good bottle of wine served as all the outlet she needed.

Within moments they had entered the palace

itself and he took her straight to the hall of mirrors, the part of the tour he considered to be the highlight by far. Judging by Izzy's reaction, she appeared to agree.

"I don't even have the words to describe this," she declared.

Chandeliers hung from the ceiling as far as the eye could see. Gold and marble statues lined the hallway atop a shiny polished wood floor.

"Royalty sure knew how to live back then."

Every part of the hall they entered was more spectacular than the last. Izzy turned on the audio guide for the tour, using the headphones they'd been handed when purchasing their tickets.

Zayn was content just to watch her as she took in all the sights, occasionally nodding to whatever she'd heard in the audio. They'd reached the princess rooms, the section of the palace that could only be described as a true testament to insane wealth and extravagance.

"Louis XV's daughters sure knew how to live in style," Izzy declared, taking off her headphones.

Zayn followed her gaze to a particularly elaborate bed in the corner of the room—Marie Antoinette's "Pink Chambers." It looked like a cotton-candy machine might have exploded in the center. A large pink bed with a draping pink canopy surrounded by pink chairs and pink furniture.

Pink. Pink. Pink.

Marie certainly had a color preference.

Izzy interrupted his musings. "This looks nothing like the room I grew up in as a teen."

Her statement brought forth myriad memories. Most of them good. Until the end.

Zayn recalled her room well; he'd sneaked in more times than he could count. Until Señor Veracruz had opened her door without knocking one fateful evening. Zayn had been in the process of crawling in through her window. She would draw her lace curtains open to indicate if she'd unlocked the windowsill for him.

Her father finally catching them had been the beginning of the end, the catalyst that had started the sequence of events that would change Zayn's life. He couldn't really blame the man—Ernesto had simply been looking out for his child. What responsible and caring father wouldn't try to intervene when he found out the town's resident troublemaker had been sneaking into the house to visit his only daughter?

Now, years later, Zayn considered himself lucky to have left her house that evening with only a tongue-lashing and a warning of dire consequences if he ever tried such a stunt again.

Aunt Myrna's reaction when she'd found out had only been slightly less turbulent. He'd received an hours-long lecture about morals and decency and honorable behavior.

That night had been one of the moments in Zayn's life that served as a metaphorical kick in the pants. Though Ernesto had certainly looked like he was barely restraining himself, he probably would have loved to have landed some actual physical kicks, as well.

"It was the best of times, it was the worst of times..." Zayn shook off the thought as they moved to the next room on the tour. Luckily for his eyes, this one's color scheme was a bit more subdued. The Princess Adelaide's chamber sported rich hues of hunter green and calming beige. And yet another intricately designed crystal chandelier hung from the ceiling, one that gave the illusion of floating candles.

Izzy trailed her fingers along the wall as she stepped farther inside. "Wow," he heard her whisper under her breath.

By the time they reached the outdoor part of the visit to tour the gardens, Zayn figured he could have done worse for his first choice of touristy destinations. The enchantment on Izzy's face was nearly tangible.

As was his ever-growing enchantment with her.

* * *

Whoever was calling her phone apparently refused to leave a voice mail and was just going to simply keep dialing until Izzy picked up. She'd been trying to ignore it, unwilling to let the outside world intrude on her fantasy outing. On a frustrated sigh, Izzy finally fished the phone out of her pocket and glanced at the screen. Zayn was across the museum's restaurant, ordering them some lunch. He said he would pick out something she would love to eat. He was fully committed to maintaining the surprise element.

Izzy felt immediately guilty when she saw the profile pic of the caller on her screen. Paula had been trying to get hold of her since yesterday.

"Hey, Paula."

Hearing her friend's familiar voice had Izzy feeling homesick all of a sudden. As much fun as she was having, she missed her beloved vineyards. She missed the harvest workers and ranch hands she considered family, the warmth of the cozy kitchen. Walking out to the mountain and inhaling the fresh air that always held the sweet aroma of the grapes was like a daily meditation for her, regardless of the weather.

But she knew once she returned, she would miss being here. And she would miss Zayn.

Izzy blinked away the thoughts and focused on her friend's familiar, soothing voice.

However, Paula sounded rather salty when she responded. "You know, Izzy... You don't call. You don't answer *my* calls. We are so going to have a chat about responsible girlfriend etiquette when you get back to the States."

There was a layer of sarcasm laced in her words, but Izzy felt guilty all the same. "Sorry, things have been rather busy."

"I forgive you," Paula immediately responded without hesitation.

"You're a gem."

"So don't keep me in suspense any longer. Did you win? Ethan and Hector looked it up, but I made them swear not to give anything away. I wanted to hear it straight from you."

It took Izzy a moment to register what she was referring to. Then it dawned on her. The awards ceremony. It felt like last night had been years ago. So much was happening so quickly.

"I'm afraid not. I lost out to a charming Argentinean farmer who only took up winemaking as a hobby just a few years ago. I'm looking forward to purchasing a bottle from his collection at the first opportunity, in fact."

Paula's heavy sigh could be heard over the tiny speaker. "Are you upset?"

Izzy had been, but she'd gotten over it. Just as she'd suspected she would. There had been other things to keep her mind occupied in the meantime. Speaking of which, she spotted Zayn off in the café queue waiting to pay for their lunch. "I'm in France, surrounded by holiday cheer and delicious food. I have nothing to complain about." She meant the words wholeheartedly, but even to her own ears her voice sounded flat and forced.

True to form, her friend picked up on the subtlety. Something in her tone must have alerted Paula's friend sensor alerts. "Uh-oh. What's going on?" she asked.

"Nothing. Everything's fine."

"Sure it is. Don't tell me, then. I'll find out eventually."

That was probably the truth, Izzy had to admit.

"Wholly unfair that you didn't win. I'm sure our cabernet could run circles around that other wine."

Izzy had to smile. "You're just being a dedicated employee and a loyal friend."

"Always. How's everything else? I want to hear all about the delicious French food. Are you enjoying the expo?"

Izzy chewed on her bottom lip, contemplating how much she should divulge. There was a fine balance between confiding in your dear friend and divulging just enough to avoid a third-degree level of questioning.

"I'm actually begging off the rest of it. We're doing some sightseeing instead." Izzy cringed as the words left her mouth. She'd slipped with the use of the one word she should have avoided.

Her friend immediately picked up on the slip-up. "*We?* Either you've met a dashing Frenchman within days of arriving or you mean to tell me that you and Zayn are traipsing around the city of romance together. Either way, I want details and I want them ASAP."

If Paula only knew. Her friend would have a field day if she ever found out she and Zayn had ended up having to share a hotel room. And all that it had led to as a result. Someday, Izzy would have to tell her. Where would she even begin?

"You can start now, by the way," Paula prompted.

Izzy didn't get a chance to respond as Zayn finished up and returned to their table with plates of food and two cups of steaming hot tea, a welcome surprise. The outside tour had definitely settled a chill into her bones. Next time she visited France in December, she'd be sure to pack something thicker than a long sweater. Zayn had clearly noticed her shivering. Hot tea would definitely hit the spot. She was thankful for it.

"We'll have to rain check, Paula. It's lunchtime here and we're about to eat," Izzy said into the phone. After saying their mutual goodbyes, she clicked off the call.

"Thought you could use this," he said, handing her one of the cups.

The man sure knew how to guess what she needed.

CHAPTER THIRTEEN

THEIR CAR HAD to circle back to pick them up once the tour was over.

Izzy stood shivering in the cold. Zayn had given her his scarf again, but it could only do so much.

"Our ride will be here soon," he reassured her, wrapping his arm around her shoulders and pulling her close against him. "Here, we'll share body heat."

They'd fallen asleep last night, worn out after a long and tiring day. She'd woken up nestled in his arms. Somehow, she'd made herself resist running her hands along his jawline, down to his shoulders, and lower and lower until he could awaken. She'd gotten up and jumped into a near scalding shower instead.

Now, with his arms around her and her pressed close to his side, desire for him shot through her body once more.

She wasn't going to be able to resist him the

next time they were alone together. It was a fact that had to be accepted. She had no willpower when it came to this man. She'd never had, had simply been fooling herself.

A glance over her shoulder and she caught his eye. The intensity in his gaze as he watched her face made her breath hitch. He wanted her, too.

Her heart thudded hard within her chest. A slow-burning ache formed in the pit of her belly and moved lower and lower still. They were out in public, for heaven's sake. A crowd of tourists hovered around them. She had to get a grip on her emotions and on her wanton desire.

Something vibrated against her hip. Zayn's cell phone in his pocket alerting an incoming call.

She had to laugh. "Saved by the bell."

But there was no hint of amusement in Zayn's eyes when he pulled out the phone and glanced at the screen. He swore a stunning curse under his breath and dropped his arm from around her.

"I have to take this. I promise it's not business. I know we're supposed to be vacationing, so to speak."

Izzy merely nodded as he stepped away to take the call. She watched as his shoulders slumped and a tightness settled over his features.

Whatever he was being told had to be some doozy of a message.

He was trembling when he returned. Alarm bells rang through her head. Was he about to have another attack? They were in the middle of the street, strangers milling all around them. Not that Zayn had actually lost control so much as his balance that day at the Eiffel Tower. Still, it had been disconcerting and frightening to watch.

That phone call he'd just received had triggered all of it.

"Penny for your thoughts," she ventured, hoping beyond hope that he might open up and tell her whatever disturbing thing he'd just heard. "It might help to talk about it."

Zayn didn't respond as their driver pulled up at that moment. He silently helped her into the backseat then waited as she scooched over before getting in himself.

As they pulled away from the curb, he slid off his coat and undid his collar. A thin sheen of perspiration slowly appeared on his forehead above his brow line.

Izzy could do nothing but take his hand in hers. He responded by squeezing her fingers tight, as if he were holding on for dear life. They sat that way in silence for what seemed to be the longest, most disquieting, ride of her life.

When they finally made it back to their suite, she couldn't contain her questions any longer.

"Zayn, please tell me what's going on. What was that phone call?"

"Nothing—it's not important." His denial wasn't even remotely believable.

"It's clearly more than nothing. Please just talk to me."

He threw his coat on the sofa and walked over to the wet bar by the side of the room near the balcony wall. He poured himself a generous helping of an amber liquid and tossed it back in one gulp. Then he poured some more.

Things really weren't looking good. Zayn appeared slightly calmer and less shaky now that they were in the privacy of their hotel room, but not by much.

Desperate for a way to help, Izzy did the only thing she could think of. She walked over, stepped up behind him and wrapped her arms around his waist.

"You can talk to me. It might help."

He slouched back against her, sending relief through her core that at least he was taking comfort in her being there next to him.

It gave her the courage and impetus to press further. He had to get this off his chest, whatever was bothering him so badly. Once she knew what was happening with him, she might have a chance to help him deal with it. She so badly wanted to give him some kind of relief, anything to take away the anguish currently flooding his face.

"What was that phone call, Zayn?" she repeated.

He took another sip of his drink and she felt him heave a deep breath against her chest. Several weighted moments passed with neither one so much as moving a hair. Gently, he eventually stepped out of her embrace and turned to face her.

"One I should have ignored."

That told her absolutely nothing. She summoned all her patience as she waited for clarification. It wasn't easy, but she felt like she was walking on broken glass here. One bad step might result in disastrous results. Finally, he spoke again after several tense moments. "That was a medical clinic located in San Antonio."

"I don't understand."

"It seems I'm the sole contact listed for one Keenan Manu Joffman."

It took a moment to process what he'd just said. When she did, Izzy felt genuine surprise clear to the bottom of her feet.

"Your father."

Zayn watched Izzy's features as the shock slowly registered on her face.

"He began trying to contact me about two

years ago." He glanced at the calendar window on his watch. "Twenty-three months ago today to be exact."

She blinked up at him. "But why? After all these years?" Then it must have registered. "You said a clinic called you. I see."

She'd always been smart and observant. He should have guessed she'd put two and two together.

"He's sick. They don't know how much longer he has. Apparently, he took another bad turn overnight. They just moved him to palliative care."

"Two years ago his calls started... You said that's right around the time your anxiety attacks began." She really was sharp as a whip. Still, he wished she wouldn't use that term. He just got a little worked up when news of his father reached him. The man had done nothing for Zayn, had been utterly useless as a parent. Now, he suddenly wanted to see his only son. Now that it was much too late for either of them.

"That's neither here nor there," he told her. "The point is I'm tired of hearing from him, tired of his attempts to contact me when it's much too late. I have better things to do with my time."

Her eyes grew wide. "I don't understand.

Don't you even want to hear what he has to say? Aren't you the least bit curious about him?"

He had to laugh. Hearing from his father was so low on his list of priorities, it barely made the list at all. He gave her a small shrug before answering. "Not even a little."

"Zayn, the man is sick."

He felt his fingers tighten on the tumbler and lifted the glass for another burning sip.

"And?" Did she have a point here? Why were they even talking about it? He wanted to push it out of his mind once and for all and take up where he and Izzy had left off back outside the château while they'd been waiting for their driver at Versailles. He hadn't imagined the desire in her eyes, nor the way her cheeks had flushed rose-red when he'd put his arm around her.

Before that blasted phone call had interrupted them and ruined what had been a perfectly enjoyable day up until then. And the evening full of passionate promise it might have led to.

All laid to waste now. Pity.

Izzy's tongue darted over her lower lip before she answered. "And you might be running out of time."

A roaring had begun to sound behind his ears. He could feel his heart rate zigzagging—

slowing down then speeding up. "Time to do what, exactly?"

"If there's even the slightest possibility that you'll regret—"

He didn't let her finish. Slamming his tumbler onto the bar so harshly half the liquid spilled out, he spun away and paced to the other side of the room. "I won't."

She looked ready to protest. Something in his expression must have given her pause. "That's absolutely your decision."

"Damn right it is."

"But it's one you should really think over carefully before arriving at any kind of conclusion."

He actually had to chuckle at her words. He spread his arms out wide. "What exactly am I supposed to weigh here? How he left when I was a toddler? How he never contacted me until he wanted to reach some kind of redemption? Or how about the way my mom took off, too, because she'd never gotten over her anger at him. Neither one of them cared that I was tossed from one relative's household to another in between foster homes until I was saddled with an elderly great-aunt who hardly knew what to do with a confused, abandoned little boy."

Even from across the room he could see the sheen of unshed tears in her eyes. She was ready to cry on his behalf. *Damn it.* This was exactly what he didn't want or need. Rehashing the past and invoking sympathy. She was the last person on earth whose pity he would want.

"I don't even know the man, Izzy."

Her lips tightened; she appeared to be chewing her words. "Zayn, what if he's dying?"

Of course, he'd thought about that possibility. In the end, what did it really change in the current scenario? In every possible way, the man was nothing more than a stranger. Zayn wouldn't even recognize him if he met him on the street.

"I don't owe him anything, Izzy. I certainly don't owe him an opportunity to redeem himself at my expense."

She swallowed. Her voice was thick and heavy with emotion when she answered. "I know you don't. But you might owe it to yourself."

Zayn stalked to the balcony door and slid it open with enough force that the windowpane next to it rattled.

"I need some air." He stepped outside, not bothering to slide the door closed behind him. A small breeze drifted in and gently rustled the curtains.

Izzy wanted nothing more than to go to him,

to pull him into her arms and gently plant a row of caressing kisses over his face and down his neck. She resisted the urge and made her feet remain planted firmly where they were. Something told her Zayn wouldn't want anything that resembled coddling or sympathy. She figured what he probably needed most right now was some space as well as the fresh air he was out there seeking.

Outside, the sound of afternoon in Paris echoed in the air. Car horns beeped, motors roared and laughter floated up from the street below. A magnificent view of the Eiffel Tower in the distance added to what should have been a charming scene straight out of a postcard.

But her heart was breaking in her chest. The man she loved was confused and angry. And he was in pain.

She ached for the unwanted little boy Zayn had been. He'd never let on back when they were together just how badly the abandonment of his parents had hurt him. And he'd never mentioned having been placed in foster homes before arriving permanently to reside with Myrna. Myrna had never wanted to talk about it, either.

What he must have experienced in those other households, she didn't want to hazard a guess. The anguish in his face when he'd talked about them just now told her more than he might have meant to.

After staring at his back for close to twenty minutes, she decided it was time. She walked over to the minifridge, pulled two frosty bottles of sparkling lemon water from the upper shelf and made her way to the balcony.

He didn't so much as move a muscle when she joined him.

Zayn stood bent and leaning over the railing, his forearms resting on the metal top rail. His head was bowed, his shoulders stumped. The entire posture was a picture of a man weary with defeat.

She held the bottle near his face in his line of vision. "I come with a peace offering."

He took it without looking at her, his gaze remaining focused on the street below. Taking the cap off with one hand, he took a long swallow. "Thanks. All that brandy was starting to burn a hole in my gut."

"Perhaps you should have drank it slower," she admonished in a clear, teasing voice. "I've been told brandy is meant to be sipped."

"I guess wealth and professional success don't necessarily lead to refinement."

"Refined is boring," she scoffed. "I've never found you to be boring, Zayn. That's meant as a compliment, by the way," she added after a pause.

He took another long swallow of his drink. "Anyone ever tell you that you're lousy at giving compliments?"

She laughed. "We all have our flaws."

"Go on then," he prompted her. "Get it all off your chest. Say what you came out here to tell me. I'll warn you, though, that I've made my decision."

She dipped her head, weighing her words. "Are you sure you've made the right one?"

He didn't hesitate with his reply. "I'm sure."

"You don't even want to hear what he might have to say?"

He shrugged, still staring off into the distance. "There's nothing he can say. Nothing will ever change the past."

"That doesn't mean you can't look to the future."

He jeered at that, his shoulders stiffening. "Hardly likely."

"And seeing him might help you to come to terms with your past. Once and for all."

"Why are you pushing this so hard?" he asked. "Why does it even matter to you?"

Ouch. Zayn didn't seem to think matters that involved him were any of her concern. Even after what they'd shared years ago. Even after their time thus far in Paris. The knowledge felt like a dagger to her midsection. One that would sting for a good while.

She made herself push past the hurt.

"I just don't want you to regret this later. You might have to live with this decision for the rest of your life."

"Are you sure that's all there is to it?"

The question gave her pause. Zayn was implying she had alternative intentions. Personal ones. Did she? Was the current situation with her own father playing any kind of role in her desire to make Zayn reconsider his decision?

Well, so what if it was? It didn't make her intent any less valid. Zayn was clearly suffering. That had to mean some kind of ambiguity. His anxiety attacks were a clear sign of that.

"Maybe you need to examine your own current predicament with Ernesto before trying to offer any kind of advice."

Bingo. She knew that's what he'd been getting at this whole time. But her temporary estrangement with her father was completely different than what Zayn was currently grappling with. "We are talking about you, Zayn. This isn't about me."

"Isn't it?" His hands clenched into fists. "Nevertheless. You grew up with a father who stuck around and cared so much for you that—"

Whatever he was about to say, he stopped abruptly.

It took a moment before he continued. "You have no idea what it's like to grow up without a dad, only to hear from a stranger decades later because he suddenly wants some kind of redemption."

"Maybe all he wants is a chance to apologize. Or to explain." And maybe a part of Zayn wanted to hear that apology. Needed to.

"I don't expect you to understand," he told her on a deep sigh.

"I'm trying to. I really am."

He shrugged. "There's no need. As far as I'm concerned, it's a moot point. No need to even talk about it." He turned then, ready to walk away and end any further discussion.

She halted him with a hand on his forearm. She'd never forgive herself if she didn't try to at least get him to see how conflicted he was.

"Zayn, don't you think there might be signs that you're not as certain as you seem? That, at the very least, you're torn about whether to see your father?"

He gave his head a shake. "I don't follow. What exactly are you getting at?"

She took a deep, fortifying breath before answering. "Your body is physically reacting to your choice with these anxiety attacks you've been having."

He suddenly went completely still. Izzy could practically feel the tension and turmoil emanating through his body. She'd said the wrong thing.

An uncomfortable silence hung in the air between them until he finally broke it. "Please don't play at being some kind of psychoanalyst with me here, Izzy. You may think you do, but you don't know me that well."

A flinch shook through her from head to toe. He was lashing out, which wasn't surprising. The knowledge didn't do much to lessen the sting of his words, however.

He delivered yet another blow before she could respond. "Why in the world would I trust you regarding this matter?" The words weren't said but she heard them all the same—he was referring to her own troubles with her father. "It's none of your concern even," he added, delivering another strike.

She wasn't strong enough to resist the innate desire to counter attack; his words simply hurt too much. She lashed out with a strike of her own.

"Somewhat hypocritical of you to bring out matters of trust, don't you think? The man who left without a word to his lover and didn't bother to ever explain himself."

His eyes clouded with disappointment. Izzy felt awash with shame as soon as she finished speaking. She should have tried harder to stay quiet, should have physically bit her lip to keep from hurling out such hurtful words. The man was in pain, and she'd just added to his suffering in a selfish fit of anger. Not that she'd said anything false. So much remained unresolved between them, no wonder the issues rose like leviathans at unguarded moments.

She'd forgotten the lessons of the past when it came to the two of them. When things were good between them, they were very, very good. But when things turned sour, they could wound each other like no one else.

He slowly shook his head, grunted an ironic laugh that held zero hint of amusement. "I should have never come back to Napa," he declared, adding another stab and proving her point. "All I wanted was to help grow that winery to its full potential. I should have known better."

She had no desire to further hurt him. But she'd be damned if she wasn't going to defend herself.

"Stackhouse is fine the way it is."

"It's stagnant, too small. Too inaccessible to scores of customers. Stackhouse could be so much more."

Izzy tried not to react to the hit her pride was taking. The implication was clear: she didn't have the kind of vision Zayn had when it came to the winery she'd devoted most of her life to.

"I've earned what Myrna bequeathed me, Zayn."

He straightened finally. "Yes, you've earned your share of Stackhouse. But you're too stuck to see it's true potential and you're too scared to try to look."

Stuck. Scared.

He'd really just used those words to describe her? And here she thought he might have some respect for her, both as a vintner and as a lover. The ugly truth now stared her down. She wasn't important enough to him in any way that mattered.

This whole week had been nothing more than a tryst, a nostalgic trip down memory lane for him.

Whereas she'd fallen in love with him all over again.

Foolish and blind to the last when it came to this man. Well, no more. It was over. She wasn't going to try to make him care for her.

Zayn Joffman was a loner and he wanted to stay that way. But she had to get one more thing off her chest before letting it go for good.

"I will tell you this. I don't think your anxiety attacks are going to get better if your father doesn't recover."

He visibly recoiled. "Please don't call them that. They're not any kind of 'attack.' I get a little shaky when I'm worked up, is all. I'm sure it happens to a lot of people."

She sucked in a deep, calming breath. She wasn't going to argue terminology or semantics with a man clearly in denial about what his physical body was trying to tell him. She'd been in some pretty deep denial herself, about so many things.

"However you refer to them, I think you need to consider that, rather than improving, they might get worse if you lose your father."

His eyes narrowed on her, a bitter smile tightening his lips. "How can I lose something I never really had?"

His words echoed through her mind like he'd shouted them from a mountaintop.

She could ask herself the same question.

She knew he was gone before opening her eyes upon awakening. The morning sun cast long shadows throughout the room. Coffee. There had to be a carafe of it nearby. The aroma tempted her nose and roused her further out of sleep. Not that she'd done much sleeping last night.

The whole evening had been an agonizing exercise in mental endurance, with her and Zayn both trying to ignore the awkward silence hanging between them. Izzy had pretended to watch an old French film with subtitles before crawling into bed early and feigning sleep. Zayn had pounded away on his laptop before slamming it shut and getting under the covers himself.

They'd stayed as far as possible on their respective sides of the bed with several feet of mattress between them.

Now she had no doubt that he was gone. For good.

She could feel it in her soul. And she felt the empty darkness his absence left behind. Her eyes began to sting and she willed away the tears. What was the point in letting them fall? Unfortunately, she hadn't learned her lesson not to play with fire the first time she'd been burned.

Rather than turning to her in his time of despair, Zayn had lashed out and pushed her away instead.

She was right, Izzy realized once she got out of bed. There was no sign of Zayn anywhere. He must have waited to make sure she'd fallen asleep then packed quietly and left. He'd bothered to bring her up a tray of coffee and croissants. One last act of indulgence right before he'd walked out of her life again.

Gingerly, she made her way over to the table and the breakfast tray. The carafe was cold now, so he must have been gone for hours. Not that it mattered; she wouldn't be able to enjoy it anyway.

A small note was propped up against the mug.

Izzy,
I'm sorry, honey. I had to leave.

You deserve so much more. And you deserve Stackhouse. All of it.

I've already instructed my attorneys to turn over my part of the inheritance and grant you full ownership.

Izzy had to put the note down before continuing. He was trying to wash his hands of her completely. Was even willing to give up his inheritance to do so. He wanted nothing more to do with her. Not as a partner. And certainly not as a lover. She'd lost him completely.

Hard to believe, but this time somehow hurt even worse than the first. For now she knew without a doubt she had never stopped loving him. And she never would.

With shaky hands, she lifted the note back up

to continue reading. The words blurred before her tear-filled eyes.

Enjoy the rest of your stay in France. The car and driver are at your disposal. Your flight itinerary is in your inbox.

Take care of yourself,
Z

He'd given no explanation of his actions or any indication of where he was headed. His words from yesterday sounded in her head. That made sense. After all, he'd told her that his affairs were "none of her concern."

She sat slowly, the note still cradled in her hand. Her eyes fell to the other two objects on the surface of the table. She'd been so focused on the note, she hadn't noticed them until now. Folded in a neat square was the scarf he'd let her borrow so often to ward off the chill over the past few days. He'd left it for her. On top of the scarf there was a small cardboard box with a satin ribbon tied around the center. Her hand trembling, she reached for it and loosened the bow.

Her breath caught when she lifted the lid.

Inside, wrapped in delicate tissue paper, was a small, handcrafted tree ornament made of clay. A miniature elf complete with floppy hat and pointy shoes—reminiscent of the ridiculous costume she'd been wearing when he'd first walked into the winery a few days ago. He must have gotten it their first night here when they'd visited the Christmas market.

The whimsical expression painted on the little guy's face wrangled a small laugh out of her.

"Oh, Zayn," she whispered aloud, her breath shaky. Emotion and loss threatened to shatter her heart. She gripped the ornament in the palm of her hand and held it close against her chest.

When had he planned to give this to her? She would never know.

If she could, she would turn back time. Find a better way to talk to him about all he was dealing with. Offer to be there to help him deal with the difficult situation with his father. Offer to be a shoulder to lean on whenever he needed. That had been all he'd needed.

She'd only been trying to help but, truthfully, she'd been so arrogant. Izzy had her own set of issues with her own dad. She hadn't spoken to or heard from him in over a year. How did she think she had the right to try to lecture or guide Zayn about his own paternal relationship?

None of it mattered. The way he'd left in the middle of the night, with only a short, perfunctory note, was a clear indication that he was finished with her. He was turning over his half of the winery. He was completely done with her and he'd been able to walk away so easily— while she was shattering to pieces inside.

She would have to accept the loss and move on, as painful as it was. They were still business partners, but he had a slew of employees and representatives who would likely be assigned to deal with Stackhouse in his stead. He, personally, wouldn't have to deal with her.

With a cry of anguish, she unfolded the scarf and held it to her face, sinking her skin into the soft fabric and breathing in the scent of him.

She didn't know how long she sat there. The morning grew brighter before she finally rose and started packing. There was no way she was going to stay here. She wanted to be home among those that she loved and in familiar surroundings while she licked her wounds.

And then it became impossible to keep the tears at bay any longer. She let them fall freely while she gathered her things.

CHAPTER FOURTEEN

"COME IN." ZAYN answered the knock on his office door without looking up from his computer screen.

Clara stepped into his office and dropped a file on his desk. "The figures you asked for."

"Thank you." He nodded to his assistant, marveling at her outfit once more. The normally stoic, serious secretary always seemed to transform into a completely different person the third week of December. She was currently wearing what could only be described as an ugly Christmas sweater complemented by flashing light-bulb earrings.

He found himself smiling at the getup.

"If there's nothing else then…" Clara began, "I was hoping to leave a little early today to get a head start on the holiday break."

That was his sign. Clara leaving from now until after New Year's day was Zayn's cue that the holidays were here and unavoidable.

The rest of his staff had already checked out. Clara was always the last. He stopped typing and leaned back in his chair.

"You're free to go. Merry Christmas, Clara. I will see you in the new year."

"Merry Christmas, Zayn." She turned to leave then hesitated in the doorway and pivoted to face him.

"Was there something else?" he asked her.

"As a matter of fact… I was wondering what you were doing for the holidays."

Zayn couldn't hide his surprise. It had to be the most personal question Clara had ever asked him.

He quirked an eyebrow at her. "Why do you ask?"

Clara crossed her arms in front of her chest. "May I be honest?"

This sounds ominous. "Go ahead."

"Well, you typically get a bit sulky around the holidays, but this year you seem more out of sorts than usual."

Wow. Things were definitely getting serious. And here he thought he'd been hiding his sour mood since returning from Paris.

"I appreciate the honesty," he lied. "As for the holidays, I'm looking forward to some nice downtime to relax and catch up on things."

She nodded knowingly. "Like work?"

"Some work, yes. And other things."

Now that he thought about it, maybe he'd go through his contact list and recruit some female company to join him. But he squelched that idea the second it popped into his head. There was only one woman he'd even hope to enjoy this time of year with. But he'd blown any chance he may have had with her, when all she'd been trying to do was help him. How many times in his life could he hurt the one person who deserved it the least from him?

Clara still stood in the doorway, studying him from across the room. He waited patiently for her to continue.

"I think maybe you're working too hard already. And if we're still being honest…" She let the words drift off, as if weighing them.

This was a side of the woman Zayn had never seen before. Clearly, she was concerned about him. Go figure.

"Yes?"

"You also seem a bit more on edge. Like you're waiting for the other shoe to drop."

Zayn pinched the bridge of his nose. So he'd been acting edgy on top of the sulkiness. Great. His professionalism was always something he'd prided himself on. Now even that was evidently slipping.

He should have seen this coming. Clara had

always been observant and aware. "I appreciate the candor, Clara. The truth is, I haven't been sleeping well."

"Care to talk about it?"

For one insane moment, he actually considered taking her up on the offer, to reach for the opportunity to get some of the turmoil of the past few weeks off his chest. To allow someone else to help him with the burden of it all, if only for a few moments. But Clara wasn't the woman he wanted to confide in.

The person who'd been there for him all along was Izzy. She was the woman he wanted to turn to right now. But he'd missed the chance to do so. A chance he'd never get again thanks to his foolishness when it came to her.

"Just have a lot on my mind."

"I see." Clara studied him a little longer and then surprised him again with her next question. "Would you like to come to my house for Christmas dinner? I'm hosting, like I do every year."

Zayn could only blink at her. Exactly how sulky and on edge had he been these past few days?

"Fairly small crowd," Clara continued. "Me, my husband, my daughter and the twins—they just turned three over Thanksgiving. And my son will be bringing his new girlfriend and her preschool-aged daughter."

Zayn didn't want to think about what her definition of a large crowd might be.

"I appreciate the offer, Clara. I'll think about it."

Another lie. It was bad enough that he'd invoked a pity invite from his assistant. The thought of actually taking Clara up on it was just too much to bear.

For a while back there, while in Paris with Izzy, he'd actually entertained notions of Christmas the way others celebrated it. With loved ones, sharing presents, eating a holiday meal together.

But he'd blown that, too.

Normal Christmases were for other people. He couldn't recall ever looking forward to the day. There certainly wasn't anything about it to look forward to now. Nothing had changed. As far as he was concerned, it was just another ordinary day. Followed by another ordinary week.

"It's an open invite," Clara told him, breaking through his dismal thoughts. She added over her shoulder as she walked out the door, "Don't stay too late. It's almost Christmas Eve."

He wasn't going to lie to her yet again, so he didn't bother answering with anything more than a nod and a smile as he watched her leave, shutting the door behind her.

No. He hadn't told her that he actually planned to stay late. The fact was he would be here until about midnight or so. Then he'd head home, heat up some leftovers and pick at the food before falling asleep. Since last week, he'd taken to falling asleep on the couch with the television blaring. Having woken in the middle of the night in a cold sweat, his heart pounding, had made the thought of crawling into bed less than appealing.

He'd told Clara the truth just now about his restless nights. For the first time ever, after returning from Paris, he'd experienced one of the episodes while asleep. And it had happened more than once since then.

Nothing like a panic attack during sleep to jolt you out of bed and have you pacing the hallways till dawn. He'd finally stopped being stubborn and acknowledged to himself that Izzy had been right to call them as such.

He couldn't ignore them any longer.

He'd been mulish about so many things while Izzy had been right about all of it. She had simply been unfortunate enough to be standing in the line of fire that was Zayn Joffman.

Your body is physically reacting to your choice.

He'd resented her in that moment for saying those words. When all she'd done was hold a mirror up for him to look at. All in an effort to ease his pain. What had she gotten for her efforts? His scorn and dismissal.

For the umpteenth time since arriving back in New York, he thought about calling her then stopped himself. The decision whether they ever spoke again was her call to make. He'd done enough damage.

Had she liked the ornament he'd bought for her their first night in Paris? Was it hanging off one of the branches of the decorated pine in the front foyer at the winery?

Maybe she'd flung it into the waste bin. She'd have every right. When he thought about the things he'd said to her… How he'd mocked her about her lack of ambition simply because she had a different vision for Stackhouse than he did. A vision his great-aunt had shared and encouraged.

Zayn threw his pen down onto his desk so hard, it splotched ink on the wooden surface. He was going to make himself crazy wondering about her.

The truth of the matter was that *he* was the one who was stuck. He was the one who was scared. All the things he'd accused her of… And holding on to anger and hurt that did nothing for him other than make him…well, sulky. He'd been in a holding pattern for so long, he hadn't even noticed he'd stalled.

No more.

Izzy had a point: he could no longer ignore things he didn't want to face. And there was one aspect in his life he had to address before anything else. Yet another thing Izzy had been right about.

Clicking the icon for the search engine on his browser, he called up contact info for Ethan Greaves, MD, and proceeded to draft an email to his old friend.

The problem with holding patterns was that they kept you spinning around in circles.

Izzy pulled into the long circular driveway that led to the entrance to the Pestaña Winery in southern Napa, the winery founded and owned by her family. The name meant *eyelash* in Spanish.

Her father liked to explain that he'd chosen the name because he'd fallen head over heels in love with Izzy's mother after she'd batted her eyelashes at him at the open market in Mexico City.

Mama always denied she'd done any such thing.

Her parents had built the winery from the

ground up and had been expanding it ever since. The place had been a source of contention between Izzy and her father pretty much since its inception. It was high time to finally put a stop to that.

She hadn't announced her visit, simply because she hadn't been certain she was actually going to go through with it. Not until she clicked on her turn signal and pulled into the parking lot.

Pleased that the lot was rather full, she got out of her car and walked to the front gate. Hector and two other employees were running a tasting outside. Papa liked to do most of the tastings on picnic tables on a veranda by the vines as long as the weather cooperated. It was certainly doing so today.

Her brother poured a rosé for the six people at his table then quickly put the bottle down. Spotting her by the gate, he gave her a wave.

"Excuse me," he told his party. "My pesky sister is here. We have to watch out for her—she's the competition." He winked after making the outrageous statement. The women sitting at his table laughed dutifully at his joke, lame as it was. Hector had the type of look a lot of women fell for. Tall and dark, though rather lanky, he somehow pulled it off. He was one of the major draws at the winery.

He strode over to her and gave her a brotherly peck on the cheek.

"Hey, sis. What brings you out here? Mama's out at the organic farm picking up ingredients for the munchies." He pointed to the picnic tables. "And I'm in the middle of a tasting."

"I actually came to see Papa. Is he here?"

Hector couldn't hide his surprise. Then his grin grew wider. "It's about time. You two are both too damn stubborn."

She ignored that. "Is he in the house?"

"He's out back, testing soil."

Izzy thanked him and took a deep, steadying breath before making her way behind the tasting area to the vines. She found her father crouched over a large silver bucket with a spade in his hand.

He looked tired. And so much older than when she'd last seen him. He worked too hard and rested too little. The kind of impressive work ethic that one would need to move from being a hired field hand from a foreign country to owning one of the most successful wineries in Napa.

She was so damn proud of him. But she would never understand him. And they would probably never see eye to eye on how to make and sell wine.

She cleared her throat by way of announcing her arrival. His eyes shot up and he did a double take when he saw her. He quickly hid his surprise.

"Hi, Papa."

"Izadora." He stuck the spade in the dirt and dug up another mound of soil.

"Isn't it kind of late to be bringing up soil samples?"

"I like to see what it's doing throughout the year. Is there something you need?"

This was it. She was here for one reason and it was too late to back out now. This was not the time for restraint. He had to know how she felt.

"Yes," she answered. "I need my father back, Papa."

His eyes shot up to glare at her. "Is that so?"

Izzy forced herself to continue. In for a penny and all that. "You have to forgive me for the decisions I've made. And you have to let me live my life."

Dropping the spade, her father pulled a handkerchief from his back pocket and wiped his brow. Suddenly he looked weary and defeated. More tired than she'd ever seen him. The silly discord between them had to have taken a toll on him, too. She, for one, was tired of it.

With a sigh, he upended two empty buckets and motioned her over. "Have a seat."

Izzy smoothed the skirt of her sundress and

did her best to sit on the too small bucket bottom. Her father sat on the other.

"Hector told me why you went to Paris. You should be proud of yourself."

With those simple words, he was telling her he'd forgiven her. Izzy felt the sting of tears behind her eyes. Her father wasn't terribly forthcoming when it came to praise.

"I didn't win in the end."

He grunted. "Nevertheless. Being nominated is quite an honor."

She sniffled, a wealth of emotion forming a brick at the base of her throat. "Thanks, Papa."

"Your brother also told me you were accompanied by Zayn Joffman on your trip."

Izzy's heart lurched at the mention of his name. Not that she hadn't been thinking about him every minute that she was awake. And when she wasn't awake. The man invaded her dreams at night.

Papa had never exactly been a fan of Zayn's. In fact, he had made it quite clear he'd wholly disapproved of the young man back when they'd been dating. In her father's defense, Zayn had not been the type of boy most fathers would have approved of.

"You don't have to worry about that," she reassured him. "We're just partners in Stackhouse. It was simply a business trip."

She prayed a punishing bolt of lightning didn't come down from the sky and strike her on the spot for such a colossal lie. The rest of her statement was true enough. She had no intention of signing and returning the paperwork Zayn's solicitor had rushed through to grant her full ownership. Myrna had left her great-nephew half of Stackhouse and that half would stay rightfully his.

But Papa had nothing to worry about if he thought Zayn was back in her life.

Her father rubbed his brow, suddenly looking tense and uncomfortable. "Well, there's something you should know when it comes to Zayn. Something I should have told you years ago."

Izzy studied her father's face. Where in the world was he going with this line of talk? The conversation had taken a turn she would have never seen coming. She'd come here to make peace with her father once and for all, to ask that he simply accept her for who she was. Yet, somehow, they were discussing Zayn.

The pieces began to fall into place with her father's next words.

"I'm the reason he left Napa, *mi niña*. I told him to go."

CHAPTER FIFTEEN

THE SHOCK OF her father's revelation reverberated in Izzy's mind the entire drive back to Stackhouse.

When she finally reached the house, she had still not fully processed the enormity of what he'd told her. That was no doubt going to take some time.

In hindsight, she really should have known. It was the only thing that made sense. Papa's interference. How could she not have guessed?

Flinging her key fob onto the side table in the foyer, she stormed off toward the tasting room. The quietest and most peaceful room on the estate, she knew being there would help to calm her. She needed to pull her thoughts together, to somehow try to think through what she'd just learned.

Zayn hadn't left her. Not really. He'd simply done her father's bidding.

Slamming the door behind her, she kicked at

a chair at the tasting table. The resounding thud of wood hitting wood echoed through the air.

"Watch it—behavior like that might lead to a lump of coal in your Christmas stocking."

She jumped at the sound of Paula's voice as her friend suddenly materialized from behind the bar.

Pulling out the offending chair, Izzy flopped herself down onto it.

"White or red?" Paula asked.

"White to start with."

Within moments, Paula had pulled out the seat next to her and produced two wineglasses and a frosty chardonnay.

"Spill," Paula ordered as she began to pour. "Does this have anything to do with your tall, dark and handsome business partner?"

Izzy sniffled. "Why do you ask?"

"You haven't been the same since you got back from Paris last week."

"It's that obvious, huh?"

Paula shrugged. "As obvious as Mr. Reyes's fake Santa beard when he drunkenly tugged at it." She comically demonstrated and earned a chuckle for her efforts. "So tell me what happened."

Izzy took a long sip of her wine, trying to gather her thoughts and put them into coherent sentences. It wasn't easy but, before she knew it, the whole sordid tale was spilling out of her.

When she finally stopped, most of the bottle of wine was gone and Paula sat staring at her, a stunned look on her face.

Izzy pushed her wineglass away, suddenly regretting the indulgence on an empty stomach. A tinge of nausea had started to whirl in the pit of her belly. "I don't know how I'll forgive him," she stated, not even sure which man she was talking about.

"You have every right to be hurt," Paula told her. "That's a lot to take in."

"And angry. So very angry," Izzy found herself admitting. The rage was making her shake inside. So much lost time.

"What exactly is making you so mad?"

Did she really have to ask? "The way I was kept in the dark… The decisions that were taken away from me… How I had no say in any of it."

"What else?"

A flash of annoyance sparked in her chest at the question, the answer was so clearly obvious. "Mostly for all the years that were wasted."

Paula took another sip of her wine. "So maybe you shouldn't waste any more time, then."

Izzy couldn't come up with a counter to that. Resignation quickly replaced irritation.

After several silent seconds passed between

them, Paula sighed long and deep. "In the end, I think there's one underlying factor you shouldn't lose sight of."

"What's that?"

"They both love you, Izzy. Your father did what he did because he wanted to keep you safe." Her friend set her glass down on the shiny, heavily polished table then turned to face her. "And Zayn loved you enough to let you go."

Izzy let her friend's words fully sink in.

A flurry of conflicting emotions churned through her core.

Anger at her father for keeping the truth from her until just now. Yet she couldn't help but feel moved at the knowledge that Papa had simply been trying to look out for her.

Relief that she finally had the answer that had so long eluded her about Zayn's sudden departure five years ago.

Admiration for Zayn in that he'd never betrayed her father's trust and divulged the truth. Though heaven knew how badly she wanted to throttle him for doing just that.

And then there was Myrna's clear attempt to once more bring them together through her last will and testament. Izzy bit back the sob at the base of her throat. Even in her final act, Myrna had managed to look out for her.

You two need each other.

Myrna's written words echoed through Izzy's head. She knew what she had to do. After all, her mentor had never led her astray yet.

Zayn figured he had to be seeing things.

He must be missing Izzy so much he was imagining her standing in the lobby of his apartment building. Wearing the elf costume, no less.

No way any of this could be real. He was definitely daydreaming or something. He had to be.

He gave a shake of his head and blinked before pulling the door open and stepping inside.

The elf was still there. An elf with Izzy's thick, dark hair and chocolate-brown eyes. And the same curves.

"Iz?"

She'd been staring at her phone screen and glanced up when he spoke her name.

"Zayn. Where have you been? I thought you'd never get home."

"I was working," Zayn answered, still not completely sure he was processing accurately exactly what was happening.

"It's Christmas Eve," she announced and then glanced at her watch. "Around ten o'clock."

He didn't know what to say to that.

She stepped toward him with hesitation. "Um, well…surprise!"

Zayn gave his head a shake to try to clear it. He didn't recall having any eggnog at the office earlier. That left only one real possibility. Izzy really was here.

"You traveled across the country to surprise me? Wearing an elf costume?"

She waved her hand dismissively. "Don't be silly. I put the costume on after I got here. I didn't board the plane wearing it or anything."

He nodded his head slowly. "Well, then it all makes perfect sense."

She looked down at the floor with a grimace. "A bit impulsive, huh?"

"I'd say."

"It seemed like a good idea when Paula and I were discussing it the other day."

Clearly, they'd been the ones having eggnog.

And then it hit him, the full-blown reality of what was happening. Izzy was here. She'd flown across the country to see him.

He didn't give himself a chance to think. Rushing across the lobby, he took her in his arms and lifted her off her feet.

"I missed you," he whispered against her hair.

Her laughter was like a healing balm to his soul. "See, this is definitely more the reaction I'd hoped for."

An older woman entered through the doors, carrying a purse, a small, furry dog poking its head out the top. She gave Izzy a look from head to toe then shrugged and walked past them.

Zayn put her down and punched the penthouse button on the elevator panel, still holding her hand. He was half afraid to let her go and risk her disappearing like a mirage.

The doors slid open a few seconds later and carried them into the hallway of his unit. Izzy stepped out before him and he flicked the main switch on the wall. Soft light flooded the apartment and the ambient fireplace at the far end of the room came to life.

Izzy pulled the elf cap off her head and squeezed it between her fingers. "I figured we needed to talk." She gestured toward her midsection. "The costume was an attempt to be playful. A way to break the ice."

She really had no idea how sexy she looked in that outfit. The look was playful, all right. But in all the wrong ways.

All that mattered was that she was here.

In a somewhat surreal moment, they both spoke at the same time, only to say the very same thing.

"I'm so sorry." Their combined apologies echoed through the air.

He stepped closer to her, took her hands in

his. The elf hat fell to the floor. "I don't know what you're apologizing for. As for me, I'm so sorry about our last night in Paris. I should have never said those things to you. Please forgive me."

Her eyes grew wide. "Oh, Zayn. Don't apologize. You saying all those things gave me the push I needed to make some hard decisions, to finally move forward with things I'd been putting off."

He could hardly believe what he was hearing. He could say the exact same words to her.

Izzy continued. "I thought my father would never forgive me. And I was too afraid to find out once and for all." She bit her lip before going on. "It's okay now. We've come to an understanding."

Zayn decided to stay quiet, as hard as it was. Talking about her father was a risky subject. He'd given his word years ago to the older man.

Izzy's next words told him the secret was out. "I know, Zayn. My father told me everything. He told me he asked you to leave because he was worried about me. Because he didn't think you were a good influence."

He pulled her hand to his lips, kissed her fingertips. Relief surged through his bloodstream. Izzy finally knew the full truth.

"I never wanted to be the cause of any kind of

friction between you and your family, Iz. That's why I walked away when he asked." Also, he'd known her father had been right to want him gone. He'd been trouble back then. Ernesto had given him the push he'd needed to take a good, hard look at the direction his life was headed.

"My father and I don't seem to need any help in the friction department," Izzy was saying. "We seem to butt heads just fine without outside help. I don't think that will ever change."

She took a deep breath before continuing. "But I know you both did what you thought was best for me. I've come to terms with that, though I have to admit it took some time and meditation."

Zayn rubbed his thumb along her bottom lip.

"There were so many times I wanted to call you after I left," he admitted. "Just to hear your voice. And to try to explain."

"Why didn't you?"

He sucked in a breath. "Because Ernesto was right. I had to get my act together before I deserved you. And I was too worried I'd be tempted to tell you the truth and break my word to him. So I put it off." He pulled her closer. "Until it felt much too late and I couldn't even figure out where I'd begin. I regret that now. I so regret not having tried."

Her eyes swam with emotion. "Then promise me there'll be no more secrets between us."

"I promise. This time I'm giving *you* my word. I'll never risk losing you again."

Izzy actually chuckled. "Well, I certainly know you're good for it."

She was so pure, so selfless. He couldn't believe he was lucky enough to be getting a second chance with her. Heaven knew, he didn't deserve it.

"I think we have a lot of lost time to make up for," she said, her breath hot against his finger at her lip. "A wise friend told me just the other day I shouldn't waste any more of it."

He nodded and pulled her closer. "Wise indeed. I agree—I think we should get started right away."

And then he didn't bother to try to think at all. Just took her lips with his own. He was panting with need by the time Izzy finally pulled away. He felt the loss like a physical blow.

Her top had crawled up several inches to reveal the luscious, tempting skin at her midriff. She adjusted the waist of the shirt and laughed. "Silly costume is just too darn small."

He gave her a wicked smile and wiggled his eyebrows. "Then we should definitely get it off you. The sooner, the better."

* * *

The next morning, Izzy woke in Zayn's sunlight-filled bedroom to the smell of hearty, rich-brewed coffee and a perfectly toasted sesame bagel smothered in cream cheese waiting for her by her bedside. She could definitely get used to the way the man she loved made sure she woke up to a delicious breakfast in the mornings. After taking a few bites and lingering in bed, she figured she should probably find him and thank him. She had all sorts of ideas about how to go about doing so.

He sat perched on the kitchen counter when she located him, his phone to his ear. He gave her a brilliant smile in greeting when he noticed her presence. She approached gingerly so as to not interrupt his call and placed a small kiss along his jawline.

"I can make it out there day after next," he was telling whoever was on the other end.

Izzy's heart sank. She was hoping they could spend the days between Christmas and New Year's with each other. But it sounded as if Zayn was making business plans. The perils of falling for a workaholic.

He clicked off the phone and reciprocated her chaste kiss with a much more passionate one. Her breath was heavy when he pulled away.

"Merry Christmas," she said when she managed to find her voice.

He grinned at her. "It certainly is."

"Who was that on the phone? Sounds like you're going somewhere."

He set the phone down with a long, weary sigh. "You're right. That was the clinic in San Antonio. I'm going to make a trip out there for a couple of days."

The ramifications of what he was saying dawned on her slowly. He'd just made arrangements to go see his sick father. A wealth of emotion swelled in her chest and she threw her arms around him.

"What made you reconsider?" she asked, still tight in his embrace.

He planted a gentle kiss to her temple. "Because you were right. The panic attacks did get worse. I couldn't ignore them or what they might mean. I couldn't risk making another bad decision that I might not want to live with for the rest of my life."

Her chest heaved against his. "Oh, Zayn."

"Any chance you're free to come to Texas with me?"

He had to know she would, that she would be with him for every step of this journey for as long as he needed her.

She hugged him tighter. "I would go anywhere with you, my love. All you ever need to do is ask."

He must have liked her response. He proceeded to show her just how much without using any words at all.

CHAPTER SIXTEEN

One year later

SHE WAS DEFINITELY better prepared for the chill this time. On this visit, she'd made sure to pack a solid, warm winter coat. Good thing, too; this year appeared to be much colder than last.

Izzy clasped Zayn's gloved hand as they walked through the square to get to the Eiffel Tower. He'd promised her he'd bring her back and he'd been true to his word.

Several moments later, when they reached the top, it had already grown dark. Slowly, gradually, lights began to come on throughout the city. They stood staring at the majestic skyline, her back to Zayn's front. Below them, Paris's lights sparkled like millions of brilliant diamonds against a dark velvet backdrop. Adding to the view, the slew of Christmas decorations all around the city and dotting the banks of the Seine.

She felt a tremble of pleasure move through

her body. How had she become so lucky? She had a career she loved, lived in a gorgeous part of the world and had the love of a man she'd more than once thought was lost to her forever.

"Cold?" he asked beneath her ear from behind, misinterpreting her shiver of delight.

She didn't correct his assumption. "A little."

"I'll have to try to fix that," he said playfully and nestled closer against her. His hot breath sent trickles of pleasure over her skin.

Their trip to France this year was so much more relaxing. None of the pressures that had existed last year had followed them this time.

Zayn had made a visit to his father just before their flight. The man was still quite ill but his condition was considered to be stable for now. Izzy knew it hadn't been easy for him, but Zayn was making a true effort to forgive and understand his father's mistakes. He made her so proud.

Now they were in Paris strictly for pleasure. No expo. No awards ceremony. No angst. Just the two of them enjoying each other's company.

Izzy released a contented sigh and nestled further into Zayn's warmth. His arms tightened around her midsection.

"I don't think I've ever seen anything more beautiful," she whispered, taking in the majestic scene below. She found herself wishing she was an artist who could somehow capture the visual on canvas, preserve it for all time. Not that it would ever leave her memory.

"I have," Zayn said pointedly, studying her profile. The way he was looking at her sent a surge of pleasure through Izzy's core. She'd been in love with him since she was a young girl, had somehow grown to love him even more since Fate had thrown them together again last December. She decided Fate had done pretty well by her for this lifetime.

"I'm hoping you'll think this is beautiful, too," Zayn said, gently turning her around to face him. In a movement that sent shock waves through her center, he pulled a small velvet box out of his pocket and knelt on his knee.

Izzy thought she'd forgotten how to breathe. Doubted she may ever remember again.

"I love you, Iz," he told her, taking her hand in his and gently removing her leather glove. "And I'd love it if you'd do me the honor of being my wife."

The ring he slipped on her finger shone as brilliantly as the magnificent lights sparkling along the skyline.

Izzy's vision grew blurry as tears of joy clouded her eyes. "Yes!" she managed to blurt out, pulling him up to stand and flinging herself into his arms. She repeated the one happy word over and over, in case there was any doubt whatsoever.

A family of tourists nearby began clapping and cheering.

Izzy couldn't help but think that Myrna was somehow watching them now, witnessing their happiness. Izzy offered up a silent thanks to the woman who had been so right to try to bring them together. Her wise words echoed through Izzy's head as they so often did. *You two need each other.*

"Merry Christmas!" someone shouted from behind them in perfect English.

It certainly is, Izzy thought, her heart near to bursting with joy in her chest. She couldn't have wished for a better holiday.

* * * * *

And if you enjoyed this story,
check out these other great reads from
Nina Singh

Spanish Tycoon's Convenient Bride
Her Billionaire Protector
Their Festive Island Escape
Swept Away by the Venetian Millionaire

All available now!